City by Night

by J.M. Frey

Third Edition published in 2020 by J.M. Frey. Second Edition published in 2017 by Short Fuse Publishing, a division of Fuse Literary, Inc. First Edition published in 2012 by Double Dragon Publishing .

www.jmfrey.net

ISBN-13: 978-1-7753402-5-6
ebook ISBN-13: 978-1-7753402-6-3

PRAISE FOR CITY BY NIGHT

"...an exceptionally fun read; I blasted through it in one sitting and loved every minute of it. A refreshing and mind-twistingly meta take on the Mary Sue convention in fanfiction, [this book] managed to subvert all of my expectations, and leave me smiling. Funny, light-hearted, and full of cracks about the tropes of genre television... is an awesome read - and the ending is amazing!"

—Sam Maggs, *The Geek Girl's Guide to the Galaxy*

"J.M. Frey deftly creates an intriguing story in CITY BY NIGHT. I enjoyed reading the experience of what can happen when fiction becomes fact."

—Linda Wisdom, award-winning author of over 100 novels

"Part sassy exposé, part heart- pounding thriller, and all about Mary CITY BY NIGHT will drop you into a world where the only thing real is courage. Highly recommended."

—Julie E. Czerneda, *The Clan Chronicles*

"With her love bite to the vampire romance genre, J.M. Frey man- ages a level of delightful satire and female empowerment that Twilight and its ilk never approach."

—Liana K., host of *I Hate Hollywood*

This one is for Karen, my fellow Anglophile and world traveler, as she was there in that little rundown pub in Bath where this story dropped into my head, and suffered gamely as I talked her through it.

This one is also for Paula Smith and Ensign Mary Sue, without whom I would not have been attracted to fan fiction and would not have learned to come into my own as a writer.

Chapters

AUTHOR'S NOTE

As you hold this book in your hands--either digitally or on paper—it has been nearly ten years to the day since I barged unannounced into Doctor Jennifer Brayton's office at Ryerson University and said: "You're going to be my thesis advisor."

This was news to her. Especially since we'd never met before. I'd only heard her name and tales of the kind of research she oversaw the night before at the graduate student's welcome wine and cheese shindig. I had decided I had better track her down immediately if I wanted to work with her, because my desired advisor for my undergrad project had already been promised to another student by the time I'd gotten around to asking her. I wasn't going to make the same mistake twice.

Well, maybe my approach wasn't quite so unexpected, because Dr. Brayton jumped up from her desk and said, "You're the student doing fanfiction and Mary Sues, right? Yes!"

I guess information on what I wanted to do had gotten around too. Post-grads. We're such gossips sometimes.

I had the distinct pleasure of sharing Jennifer as an advisor with several other students at the time—most notably a fellow author and Canada Reads finalist. It was sometimes hard to get a meeting with Jen, but every wait was worth it.

For my project, we decided that I would write a thesis project essay about the importance of self- representative avatars for the development of new writers, and how fans use stories where they or their avatars enter a fictional world to explore not only that world, but also their self-identity and sexuality. In the worlds of fan fiction, this is known as a "Mary Sue." The term was coined in 1973 by Paula Smith in her short satirical story A Trekkie's Tale, and has since taken on derogatory connotations. "Mary Sue" is now a catchall term for protagonists who are too perfect to be believable to the audience, and too preoccupied with sex and appearance. Though it often only applies to female characters, rarely the male ones that often occupy mainstream media texts.

My project was in part an effort to reclaim "Mary Sue" for the fan fiction writers who used the trope, and to point out that many of the people who did were deploying it in interesting, self- reflexive ways that even they probably weren't aware of.

To do accompany the paper, I decided that I would also submit some of my own early Mary Sue Fan Fiction. And as a contextual contrast, write another new Mary Sue story that demonstrates how powerful and important a Mary Sue can be when they're written deliberately. And to do so, I wanted to create a whole fictional world for my Mary to occupy.

That story eventually became The Dark Side of the Glass, a novella that was first published, after my thesis was complete, with Double Dragon Press. You're holding now the updated and polished version City by Night.

Not much has changed in the book—some references to social media and online archival sites, mostly—but the opportunity to revisit the tale and clean up the text a bit was thrilling. Not to mention, the fantastic new cover the story got! (Thanks, Archia & Rodney!)

What really struck me during the re-read though, was the reminder of how much fun writing this story had been.

I love vampire tales. I have ever since I read *Interview with the Vampire* for the first time. That was right around the time that one of the biggest Prime Time stories airing on Canadian television was *Forever Knight*, an episodic drama about an eight- hundred- year- old vampire who regretted his centuries of mayhem and bloodshed. He had joined the ranks of the Toronto Police Force in order to atone for his sins.

The 1980s and 1990s were rife with similar plot lines. Vampires who find their humanity and work to repay society, or never lost their humanity to begin with and use their powers for good. It's safe to say that this book came from many, many hours of watching and reading the television programs and novel series of my youth that made me fall so in love with the vampire myth, fanfiction, and the vampire-as-detective-tropes, (all of which I still desperately adore): *Dracula: the Series, The Vampire Files, Angel: The Series, Dark Shadows, Moonlight, Nightwalker,* and *Blood Ties.*

So it made sense to set this book in a world like that – sexy brooding vampire, evil domineering master, innocent plucky side-kick, and a world where creatures bump the things that go bump in the night right back. I satirize because I care.

In the years it took to write the project, and this story, Jen guided me through many other papers and presentations. Even though technically she was only supposed to be my advisor on my thesis, she became my mentor and idol. It was she who helped me not only perfect my abstract and then my paper for my first academic conference in Cardiff, Wales (where I spoke on the hidden Canadian genesis of the hit TV series *Doctor Who* to people who actually worked on the show—my fave screenwriter Rob Sheraman, chief Dalek operator and Big Finish Audio director and producer Barnaby Edwards, and later at a rowdy pub event where we watched Wales absolutely cream Canada in the rugby, Torchwood actor Gareth David Lloyd.)

After my thesis was completed, and my defense done, Jen became my friend and hang-out buddy as I navigated the post-graduation world of Toronto. When I told her that my agent had placed *The Dark Side of the Glass*, she was so thrilled we sat out on a patio drinking sangria until we had sunburns. Weirdly appropriate for a celebration of a vampire book, I guess!

When it was decided that I should write an introduction to this novella, the first thing I thought of was Jen, and our time together in her horribly lit office, crammed with pop culture scholarship books and action figures, and the way we would talk WoW, and giggle over fanfic, and plan to meet up with one another at conventions. For me, this book, that thesis project, and Dr. Brayton are insolubly intertwined, a braid of inspiration, creation, and investigation.

And now, here we are, a full ten years later.

We have since drifted apart as Jen moved on from Ryerson, but those years under her tutelage, the years that produced this novella, remain cherished. So much so that you'll see I dedicated *The Forgotten Tale*, book two of the Accidental Turn series, to her. But I know she's pleased as punch that this book is getting a reprint, and so in addition to the first dedication that this book had upon printing, let me add:

To Dr. Jennifer Brayton, who encouraged a young woman that it was okay to question, and investigate, and learn. This book is not only for you, but also from you.

J.M. Frey
Toronto, Ontario

City by night

Chapter One :
Concerning Rabbit Holes and All That

When Mary comes to, she is lying face down in the grass beside the road.

Her first conscious thought, beyond *Ow ow ow,* is *How long have I been lying here?* Followed closely by *Ouch* and *Am I really so unimportant that nobody has helped me?* and *Ouch* and *Where am I?* Followed again by *Ouch* as she tries to get her hands under her shoulders and push herself onto her knees.

Rain has pooled in her upturned left ear. Her toes are frozen. Everything aches. Her head throbs. Her knees and her palms burn. Her left arm and left leg are bleeding, both from jagged gashes right above the joint that look way, way grosser than anything she's ever seen people sporting after a visit to the Effects Makeup trailer. There's grit in the long cut, and when Mary flexes her fingers, she can feel the sickening grind of grains of dust against her muscles. It feels disgusting, the way that frogs squashed by a little boy's shoe is disgusting, with that sort of oozing pop.

The Craft Services van that hit her is nowhere to be seen. The studio is gone, too, even though she was pretty sure she hadn't run that far. Something warm and salty stings her left eye.

She's on a street she doesn't recognize, at night, with streetlamps that only mostly work. They cast an amber glow over the glistening pavement, so perfectly moody that it looks like something out of a cinematographer's wet dream. There's grass between the sidewalk and the road, and it's wet from a storm that must have passed over her while she was unconscious, if her wet hair and ear are anything to go by. The air smells of...nothing.

Nothing at all. For reasons Mary can't fathom—reasons which make her heart beat faster, her shoulders ratchet up to her ears—this unnerves her. It's unnatural.

There's no one on the barren street. It's a strangely harmonious mix of residential and storefronts made out of the converted ground floors of houses, all dark and closed up for the night. There is, by some strange cosmic luck, or fate, or universal synergy, a phone booth less than a block away, on the corner. Mary hasn't seen a phone booth in years, but she doesn't own a cellular phone herself because she never wanted to be distracted at work. She hates her coworkers when they tap away with their thumbs, instead of paying attention to who is going in and out of the studio gate like they're being paid to do.

It takes Mary a few minutes to get upright. She is reminded unpleasantly of the cliché about the wounded gazelle on the Serengeti: weak and tottering, but too afraid of attracting the wrong attention to bleat for help. Her head throbs again, and then a very stupid realization bubbles up to the surface of her muzzy brain: she is alone.

Totally alone.

There is no one on the street. There doesn't even seem to be anyone in the *houses*. The Craft Services van driver, her boss, and her co-workers have all just *abandoned her*, left her for dead on the side of the road. Clearly, nobody came after her. Nobody even stopped to make sure she was *alive*, as far as she can tell.

That says a lot more about how they think of her than Mr. Geary's horrible insults about her scripts. *The ungrateful...jerky jerks!* Mary thinks, clutching at the gash on her arm.

She has given *City By Night* two goddamned years of her life. She just wants the show to love her *in return*. Is that so very much to ask?

Apparently, it is.

Anger fuels her enough to get her over to the phone booth, helps her exchange pain for momentum. Clutching at the scarred metal frame of the door to stay upright, she stares in stupid incomprehension at the coin slot for a second. Her left hand dips unconsciously into her empty pocket, which is its own sort of special agony. She nearly cries when she realizes she has no quarters. It takes her a few more fuzzy, swimming moments to realize she can probably make emergency calls for free. Hopeful, she

3

fumbles up the handset and dials zero. The operator—female and far too perky for Mary's dark frame of mind—comes on and asks what she needs or where she would like to be connected. "I need help," Mary says into the handset. She can practically hear the operator frowning, because, *duh*, why else would she be talking to one? "I was...I think I was hit by a car. A van. Whatever."

"Holy sugar!" the operator says, all professionalism thrown out the window. Mary wonders if the operator calls her husband *punkin*. "Stay where you are, ma'am. We're tracing the call and an ambulance is on the way."

Mary winces; she's too young to be called "ma'am" just yet, and it's another dig at her self-esteem that she really *does not need* today. It's pretty thoroughly dug already.

"Thanks," she says, and lets the handset clatter out of her grip, relieved because it was pressing into her road burn. She slumps down the side of the phone booth to wait. She folds bruised elbows over bruised knees and rests her head back against the Plexiglass and tries to stay awake. She read that you're not supposed to go to sleep if you've hit your head, and she thinks getting smacked in the skull with a Craft Services van counts. The cord for the phone handset isn't long enough to reach all the way down to her ear, so she just lets it dangle, detachedly amused by the way the operator's voice is squawking out at her. She's pretty sure that she's probably in shock. She's also pretty sure that the fact that she's in shock isn't supposed to be funny, but she realizes belatedly that she's giggling all the same.

Hysteria makes Mary drift for a while. She's aware of closing her eyes, of replaying every time Crispin Okafor winked at her from the back seat of his car, the way she received the cast photo poster after the Season One wrap party, already signed with what she assumed at the time was a personal message. She thinks about how much she threw herself into the show, and how she's never seemed to notice or care that she has been bouncing off of brick walls.

It's a sucky thought. She stops giggling and lets herself be sad for a little while.

She might have even cried, but by then, her head is pounding and her whole body is like one stiff, hot rip. She thinks maybe the wetness on her face is tears, but it could also be rain, or blood; it's hard to keep track, especially when the liquid feels so warm, and her skin is getting so cold.

She wonders if she should be mad for a bit, just to change things up, keep her life interesting until the ambulance arrives, but she isn't sure whether she should be madder at the crew or herself for being so gullible. That spirals her back down into depressing aching sadness again, so she decides to stay there.

And somewhere in all of that, she thinks she sees Crispin Okafor. Crispin—the damnably beautiful lead actor who knows just the right way to smirk at a paparazzi camera, what angle he should hold his head and shoulders at—is sticking his face into the phone booth. He's dressed in his costume; that black leather jacket that Richmond DuNoir favors (whose style Mary has copied), in the signature red silk shirt that makes his smoky dark skin take on the depth of velvet, that fake look of honest concern.

"Miss?" he asks softly. "Miss, are you all right?"

"Fuck off, Crispin," she says back. At least she thinks she says it. It might come out just as a slur. Her mouth feels full of marbles and cotton now, and it's getting harder and harder to do anything as simple as moistening her lips. Of course, Mary very rarely swears, so it could be that, too.

She feels like this is an appropriate time to start, though.

"Miss, I think you're pretty badly hurt."

"Go away," she says, miserably. "You're the last person I want to see right now."

He startles visibly, dark eyes becoming dramatic white spots on his shadowed face. *Overdone*, she thinks. *You're trying too hard to emote. Retake.*

"You know me?" he asks.

"Seriously, I said go away."

He looks like he wants to argue with her, but cuts himself off, halted by the sudden approaching wail of sirens. The ambulance screeches to a halt beside her, washing the interior of the phone booth red and blue by turns, painting the already pale skin of her arms with deathly tints: blood-red and dead-flesh-blue and back to skin-colored before alternating again. Crispin is gone between flares, melting artistically into the darkness.

Mary's head starts throbbing worse in the flashing light, and she is pretty sure she's going to vomit any second now. She wishes Crispin had hung around long enough so she could do it on his goddamned shoes.

*****

Mary is a parking production assistant on *City By Night* when the television crew is on location, which is pretty much for every exterior shot. She thinks her job is totally awesome because, according to her, *City By Night* is pretty much the best show that has ever been on the air. She gets up at four o'clock in the morning every day, and she doesn't have weekends, but that's okay, because she gets time off during the hiatus. Before she leaves her apartment, she has a cup of coffee and a bowl of granola, and bundles up into her fleece vest and faux leather jacket, even in August, because the air blowing off Lake Ontario can be *cold* before the sun rises. Well, that and because it makes her look like Richmond. She touches the faces of the actors on the poster pinned to the back of her front door, smiling or snarling according to their characters, and runs her fingers over the slightly raised silver sharpie scrawl:

Mary, couldn't do it without you!

She catches the streetcar, rumbling red pieces of crap that Toronto can't seem to get to stop squealing, and goes down to the lakefront studio to pick up her daily stack of small orange traffic cones. She picks up the day's map and takes the city transit to the location, or uses up one of her monthly allotments of taxi chits if the transit isn't convenient. By five-thirty in the morning, she has the blocks all staked out: this much space for the actor's trailers, a side street over there for Hair and Makeup and Effects, that parking lot for everyone's vehicles and drivers, and the Craft Services van, and of course, the street on which they are going to be shooting. Sometimes, in the cold hush of pre-dawn, she walks down that street and imagines that she is an extra in the shot, or perhaps a guest star explaining her supernatural mystery of the week to the hero.

Morning commuters complain. They wave their middle fingers at her when she explains patiently that the city has leased the property to the show for a few days, a week at most, and it's not her fault that they didn't inform their patrons ahead of time. "Besides," she asks them, "won't it be exciting to see your regular parking spot on TV?" The commuters don't usually agree.

"*City by Night*?" they shout. "That show's a piece of shit!"

The citizens of Toronto like the money that the film industry brings in well enough; they just don't like the inconvenience of the actual filming itself. Mary thinks that her job is glamorous, even on—especially on—the days when working in television is at its *least* glamorous. She protects the lot; keeps out people desperate to park in the wide empty spaces, makes sure that only the crew she knows by sight, or with the correct paperwork, can get in. And it is wonderful. The horrible burnt coffee from the Craft Services van is wonderful; the way she can't feel her toes and fingers and the tip of her nose is wonderful. Working long hours is wonderful. Better than wonderful.

It's *television*. It *has* to be.

Mary knows that her job is important, though the production team never stops to tell her so, *because* they never stop to tell her so. They are too busy. It is her job, her very important job, that lets the creative people get on with their busy days, their own hectic art-making. If it wasn't for her, they would waste hours and hours every single day just trying to find parking spaces, and then the show would never get made and then the network would pull their funding and it would be cancelled. Worse than that, some school bus on a field trip might pull up and take the precious principle's trailer parking spot, and nobody wants a zillion kids screaming around the set while the transport coordinator is trying to shout at the driver about permits.

Mary's job is vital.

Every day at around noon, the Craft Services van starts to make greasy burgers, crisp fries, and wilted salads. At around three, the director and camera chief arrive to survey what the lighting and rigging crew, set decorators, and construction crews have spent the day preparing. At about three-thirty, the principles arrive. Crispin, teeth like pearls against his dark lips, always winks at her behind his equally dark glasses when he goes by. She's certain of it.

After all, he signed her poster personally. He couldn't do it without her.

Around the time when the sun starts to set, a different PA comes to relieve her, and Mary is done for the day. She doesn't like the other PA—he's a panderer. He waves and says "hi" and chats with the people already on the lot. Mary is sickened by the way he tries to climb the ranks by bringing donuts, or coming in twenty minutes early to hang out with the incoming crew, instead of just buckling down and doing his job. When promotion time comes, she knows that hard work wins over fake geniality any time.

Mary goes home, bumbling along on the streetcar with the rest of the exhausted, rude commuters. She has thought about getting a cat; she'd like someone to say "hi" to when she comes home. But she is afraid that her long hours would be unfair to any animal, and so she got a ficus instead. She says, "Hello, puss" and pats its topmost leaves as she walks in the door, and only sometimes giggles at her own silliness.

The show airs Thursdays at 8 p.m., so on those days, she goes swimming in her building's pool beforehand, makes a nice dinner, opens a bottle of wine, and watches *City by Night*. She only turns the TV off after she sees her name in the credits.

The first time the show aired its pilot episode, she was on the phone with her mother. They watched it together, the whole hour (forty-eight minutes plus commercials). Her mother screamed when Mary's name scrolled by.

The other nights of the week, Mary goes online straight after coming home. She checks her email, scrolls through the online communities about the show, checks out what is trending on Twitter, and reads some *City By Night* fan fiction. She's always been tempted to write some of her own, but she's employed by the program, so she's never sure if writing fan fiction would count as a breach of contract.

Besides, Mary is saving all her story ideas for the production team.

Mary writes scripts. She knows how they're supposed to look; she's seen the real scripts before. At least, she's seen the pages that deal with what she's supposed to stake out.

Mary gives the production team one script a month.

She always wraps it in a brown production envelope and slips it under the executive-producer-slash-showrunner's office door when she picks up her cones. The first Monday of the month, every month. He might be worried if she didn't, after all. Might think she isn't feeling well. They haven't made any of her stories, yet, but there's been a few lines, sprinkled in here and there, that she's sure were hers first. She doesn't demand a cut of the writer's cheque, though, because she is just grateful that they'd used what she's written, just grateful that she gets to work on a show that she loves so much, which has such a large and loyal and interesting fanbase.

Mary goes to the science fiction and fantasy media conventions. In Toronto, there's one every five or six weeks, so she's never starved for choice. She doesn't get in line to get an autograph from the principles, though. That would be weird. She's certain they'd recognize her. She thinks she probably wouldn't have to pay, might even get her own nametag saying "guest" if she told the organizers who she is. But she likes the ability to walk around unrecognized, to be able to observe and overhear the fans.

At 9 o'clock, when the show is over, or she's finished reading, or she's back from the convention, she goes to bed and smiles in her sleep because she loves her job. She really, really does.

At least, she used to.

*****

Mary is startled back to herself when she manages to get a good look at the city crest patch on the arm of the paramedic. She is in an ambulance, strapped to the gurney so she can't roll around the interior of the box, though she doesn't remember getting onto it. The paramedic is beside her, threading an IV tube of some sort of clear solution—saline or morphine or something—onto the needle he just stuck into the back of her hand.

"Huh?" Mary says out loud. She tries to strain her head up to get a better look at the patch, because she *knows* that crest, the stylized waxing moon, and the made up skyline. She's seen it before. Lots. *Daily*, even.

The other paramedic, the pretty woman who looks like every extra ever that Mary has had to wave through a checkpoint, pushes her back down. "Lie still, hon," she says in a forced, stilted way. "We're almost at the hospital."

"What hospital?" Mary asks, feeling suddenly frantic. But frantic is exhausting, so she breathes out and concentrates real hard on not straining against the safety restraints of the gurney. "Where am I?"

The paramedics exchange a glance over her vulnerable body. Mary can all but hear the tense music building in the background; the familiar saxophone flourish that indicates that this week's mystery has begun.

"Night City, hon," the woman says. "Where else?"

Mary wishes suddenly that she was a fainter. That she could gulp air prettily and flop backward, and the world would just go away for a little while. At least, for as long as it would take for all of this to start to make sense. That would make all this so much easier to deal with. Instead, she relaxes back onto the gurney and tries not to think too hard.

"Night City," she repeats. "I've gone crazy. That's it. I worked too hard. I've had a psychotic break. My mother was right. Oh, God."

The paramedics say nothing. Maybe they're not allowed to improvise. Maybe they can't speak unless a character carrying the plot asks them a question. Maybe they can only react.

"This is a joke, right?" Mary asks. "This can't really be real."

"Why not?" the man asks.

"Because Night City is fiction. It's Toronto, dressed up to look like New York." Mary grimaces. "Only it comes across like Detroit because the budget doesn't allow for getting permits on the nicer streets!"

The paramedics exchange another glance.

"Lie still, hon," the woman says. "We're almost at the hospital."

"You said your line already," Mary snarks. Like swearing, she generally refrains from snark, but she can't seem to control her mouth. Probably because of the shock—things that she normally holds onto tightly keep flying out of her, and she doesn't know how to stop it.

Worse, she's afraid she might actually mean them.

Then everything gets fuzzy; somebody has turned on the morphine drip. She's not sure if that's better or worse than fainting.

*****

This is the script, she's certain that this is the script. They are going to make this one, for sure. They haven't made any of the others, but *this* one is perfect! She re-read it one last time before she went to bed. There are small spelling corrections made in Liquid Paper and neat, careful strokes of her black ball point pen. She's even indicated which pages were rewrites by printing them on canary, rose, or robin's egg blue pages, as fitting the number of versions they went through.

Mary walks to the door of the executive-producer-slash-showrunner's office and stops. The light is on, spilling out from the cracks in the ill-fitted jambs in buttery slices. He has never been in his office when she dropped a script off before. She hesitates.

Inside, she hears voices.

"Every first Monday," one of them says, and she knows that voice: that's him, the executive-producer-slash-showrunner, Mark Geary. "Just wait. Two years we've done this show, and she drops one off every first Monday, without fail."

Mary's chest swells with pride. He is *waiting* for her scripts now. How fantastic! She doesn't even wait to see how the other voice replies. She is elated, so buoyant that her hand seems to lift itself. She knocks.

In the office, someone says, "Shhhh!" And then the executive-producer-slash-showrunner opens the door.

"Hiya, Mister Geary," she says. "Mark." She holds up the brown envelope, grinning. "Right on time!"

"It sure is, Mary," he says, and he is grinning so hard, and his cheeks are so red that it looks like he'd been laughing a lot recently. She wonders if it was because he thought of a really great joke for a script. That would be cool. He smells a little bit of scotch, but Mary ignores it. Mr. Geary would never be so unprofessional as to drink at work. That isn't something that happens on *her* set.

She tries to peer around Mr. Geary, but he is filling up the whole door, keeping his body tight between the jamb and the knob. He is trying to hide her from whoever is in the office with him, Mary realizes.

Maybe he wants to keep his mystery writer a secret from them! It is an exciting thought. It makes her toes wriggle in her boots, and the skin along the back of her neck prickle.

She jiggles the envelope, because Mr. Geary hasn't reached up to take it yet. She thought he'd be more impatient, that he'd snatch it right out of her hands like a hungry wolf. He was just being polite, yes, that's what it is. Mr. Geary has always been very polite.

"Right, right," Mr. Geary says. He wipes his palms on the thighs of his jeans and takes the envelope. "Thanks, Mary. Have a good morning."

"You too, Mister Geary! Mark, I mean! I, uh, I'll see you later. On set? Right?"

"Sure thing, Mary," he says. He is grinning really hard again; maybe he has just been anticipating getting time to read her new script.

"I won't keep you away from it," she says, making an aborted gesture toward the envelope. The motion feels funny and awkward even to her, so she stops so it won't become too prominent. He has the script rolled up in his hands like a bludgeon.

15

He closes the door before she is all the way out in the hall, and it makes her happy. *He must be really eager this month!*

She starts to walk down the hall, aware of the voices hushed in anticipation. When she gets far enough away, she stops. She reaches down quietly, takes off her boots and tiptoes back, crouching down beside the jamb to listen. Even she is not above some much needed ego stroking.

There is the crinkle of the envelope being opened, the delicious dry slide of paper on paper, and then a whispered murmur. "I'll be damned," Mr. Geary says. "I was right."

"What?" asks another voice, and Mary is stunned to realize it is Crispin; Crispin Okafor, the lead actor, coming to work ten hours early just so he can read her scripts. Or maybe staying late. Mary has to press a fist into her mouth to keep from squealing with excitement.

"This title," Mr. Geary says.

"Yes?" And that is the chief director's voice. Director and actor and showrunner, all at once!

Yes? Mary thought.

"It's even *worse* than the last one."

Crispin guffaws. The Director whistles. Mary swallows hard.

"God, she just won't stop," says Mr. Geary. "We haven't made one damned script, but she keeps writing them. We can't even return them 'cause she never leaves a forwarding address, and she personally picks up all of her paycheques. Look at this; another dumb original character! As if we have the cash to hire another wannabe starlet! God, if she wasn't so damned good at what we actually pay her to do, she'd have been fired an age ago."

Mary swallows again, and it tastes sour.

"At least she has passion," says Crispin, and he sounds... cynical. He doesn't sound anything like the deep-voiced, honest, earnest man that he plays. Or the enthusiastic, grateful actor he is in his interviews. "At least she's not *bored*."

"Oh, shut up," says the director. "Whose fault is it that you signed the three year contract? Not mine."

"*I* didn't know the show was going to be so vapid," Crispin snapped back. "What's she got here? Maybe it won't be half so dull as what I actually have to say." There is the rustle of paper and a short silence. Mary can hear her heart pounding in her ears, and it is speeding up. "Nope, this dialogue is actually worse. Who'd have thought *that* was possible? Maybe you *should* hire her as a screenwriter— this will guarantee the series would tank. Why won't they just cancel us already? This is hell."

"Just stick it out for twenty more episodes," Mr. Geary says. "Then we'll have made enough money back on this genre garbage from all the douchey little goth kids."

"And production insurance," the director says, and his voice is gleeful.

Mary's heart starts pounding so hard she has to press the heel of her palm against her chest to make sure it stays inside her skin.

Mr. Geary snorts. "You could actually mount that theatre production that you've been moaning about."

Crispin says, "I had an idea about the swordfight—" But Mary doesn't hear the rest.

What she does hear is the distinctive sound of a thick sheaf of papers thunking into the bottom of a metal wastebasket.

She stands up, forgetting that she still has her boots in her hands. Her fingers are shaking too much to hold them, and they go crashing to the ground.

Mary is horrified. She is mortified. Mary *hurts*.

She *loves City by Night*. She *loves* the haunted, tortured Richmond DuNoir, the heartless villain Antonio, the innocent but spunky street kid Sherri. She *loves* the romance of eternity, the juxtaposition between the darkness of the vampire soul and the light Richmond so yearns for. She loves the way Richmond throws himself into each mystery, the way he feels he owes the world his goodness because so much bad has been done to him. She loves all the little mysteries and all the flashbacks. She *loves* the rich historical costumes. She *loves* her job, and she loves everything about the show, and she *hates* that everybody who makes it doesn't.

They are mean for teasing her. Mean for not taking her seriously. Mean for leading her on. Mean for not making her scripts when she knows, she *knows* that they're exactly what the show needs to revive it, she *knows* that her scripts are exactly what the fans want. Mary's read their fan fiction and talked to them at the conventions and lurked on their message boards. She knows because she is a fan, too.

And that, it seems, is more than *they* can say for themselves.

She thinks that it is not *fair.*

Her heart breaks to hear that Crispin and Mr. Geary don't care about their fans at all. That they *hate* them.

It is not fair that people who dislike the show are responsible for making it. It is not fair that they *thought it up* and still hate it. It is not fair that they don't appreciate their fans the way Mary does!

So she runs.

She doesn't pick up her traffic cones at the little office. She doesn't even bother to pick up her boots. She thinks she hears the door to Mr. Geary's office open, thinks she hears Crispin call her name. "Mary!" But she doesn't stop to check.

She just wants to get away.

She runs. She knows that her face is hot and the tips of her ears are burning, and there is something searing and golf-ball sized pressed against the back of her larynx, against the backs of both of her eyes. She runs. She knows that her hands are shaking, even as she pumps them in fists by her side.

She runs. Away from the lot, away from the show, away from the embarrassment. She doesn't know where she is running to with no shoes, only that it is down the hall, out the door. She runs into the parking lot in her sock feet on a cold, wet March morning, onto the sidewalk and partway across the road.

She runs.

She doesn't see the Craft Services van coming round the corner on an illegal red light turn. She smells the grease, familiar as her own shampoo, but she doesn't see the van.

Not even when it is too late.

Chapter Two :
A Prince Who is Less than Charming

Mary wakes up in the hospital feeling indignant. There was no need to drug her into oblivion just because she called their existential reality into question! All she can smell is the heavy yellow reek of iodine and the sickly sweet nothing-smell of industrial cleaners. It's awful, and a damn sight better than the nothing-nothing of outside. Back there it felt like someone had just...*forgotten* that the outside world should have ambient smell, too. Hot pavement and car exhaust, old garbage and freshly cut grass, rain on the sidewalk and street meat.

The heels of Mary's hands, elbows, and knees sting with the slight burn of antiseptic. They're covered in bandages.

Something itches and pulls along her left forearm and she turns her head. She manages to ruck up the sleeve of her hospital gown enough to see that there's a line of stitching there, and a matching one on the thigh of her left leg. She reaches up, and yes, there are a few small stitches right above her left eyebrow, too.

Fantastic. Great.

Indulging in a swear twice in one day would call for something really extraordinary. She considers carefully and decides that this is something really extraordinary. Licking dry and stinging cracked lips, she hisses out: "Fuck."

Mary wouldn't drop the F-bomb for anything less than...well, whatever the *fuck* this is supposed to be.

She lays back and sighs, and hopes that her trip in the ambulance and the patches on their paramedics arms had just been a hallucination. That's all it *could* be. She hit her head; a *van* hit her head. She was imagining it all. Too much *City by Night* and not enough social life, her mother would say.

Mary has friends outside of the show, friends from the film school she graduated from three years ago. Sometimes she hangs out with them. Even though the last time was months ago and there was a flu bug going around that kept half of them away, and then a few others had forgotten about prior commitments, and someone's dog got sick... But she does have friends.

Doesn't she? She can't remember the last time she saw any in person. Her birthday, maybe. But they're still her friends, even if they're all too busy with their new careers, just like her. That's what happens when you graduate.

When you get a job in your field. When you're *in demand*.

She scrubs her eye with her hand and the sting reminds her just where she is. Only...she can't really be here. It's a... yes. A dream, yes.

Except that the illusionary hospital room she's in is way too nice and way too private to be anything except a film set. Real hospitals never give patients who arrive on the universal healthcare bill private rooms, not ones like this. Mary gives in to the urge to look up, to check that the room actually has a ceiling instead of a row of pipes suspended on thick cables for the mounting of hot, heavy lights. There is only a row of fluorescent lights, turned off, and a solid ceiling painted a slick, calming cream. A lamp glows golden on the bedside table, an island of warmth in the darkness that throws the rest of the room into a sort of gloomily ambient perfection of chiaroscuro.

What the hell? she thinks, and then says it out loud. "What the hell?"

"Hello again, Miss," a voice replies, and Mary yelps at the unexpected words and nearly gives herself whiplash yanking her head around. "You're awake."

The window is open. It looks out onto a city skyline that she has never seen in any travel brochure, but knows the way that she knows Toronto's. Intimately. She has walked amid its imaginary canyons of cement, and steel, and glass. She has helped build them.

There is a man seated on the window frame. She can see his silhouette against the faint skyscraper lights and a sunset that is revoltingly perfect. There is no telltale criss-cross of shadows that would indicate a fire escape for him to climb up.

They're on at least the fourth or fifth floor, Mary realizes. Maybe higher.

"Hello," she says back, and her mouth is very dry. Her voice croaks.

The shadow stands up and walks toward her. Mary closes her eyes very, very tight. She hears the sound of water being poured into a dinky paper cup, the funny plastic clink of the pitcher being set down on the bedside table, feels the press and intimate outline of a hand on her shoulder—but none of the warmth—the touch of the rim of the paper cup on her bottom lip. She sips because the cup is there and insistent. It moves away and she still does not open her eyes.

"This isn't real," Mary says. Because she recognizes the voice, the silhouette. Of course she does.

"It's very real. I'm afraid you were hit by a driver who didn't stay at the scene. You've been asleep all day."

"That's not what I mean," Mary says. She fists her hands in the sheets, feels the uncanny tug of the stitches in her skin, the shift of the needle in the back of her right hand. She feels exposed lying down like this, unable to defend herself. She tries to sit up, and failing in that, to find the remote that will make the bed rise.

The man chuckles. "It would be easier if you opened your eyes, Miss."

"No," Mary says. "That would make this...make it real."

The man sighs, sounding amused, and then the bed starts to lift behind her back, the soft whirring buzz drowning out the pound of her heart in her own head; he clearly realized what she had been looking for. She can sense him standing by her head, but she can't feel his body heat or smell his skin. She can't even smell his deodorant or cologne. She doubts he is wearing either. He's not making any noise, no minute shuffles, no extraneous gestures, nothing of the flickering, ever moving flutters of *life*.

"You know why I'm here, then?" the man asks. His voice is closer to her ear now, and she assumes he's taken a seat in the absurdly plush visitor's chair.

"Maybe?" Mary squeaks. "Just...you're Crispin, right? Crispin Okafor? And I'm not crazy?"

"Miss..." the man says reproachfully. Mary finally can't deny the urge to open her eyes, to keep him in her sights, because being unable to track him by sound is terrifying in a sort of monkey-brain, I-don't-know-where-the-predator-is-hiding kind of way. He's shaking his head slowly, sadly, that beautiful little flop of black hair that she always found endearing flicking back and forth on his forehead.

"You're Richmond DuNoir." It's not a question, and Mary feels silly. Silly and scared, because *how* can this be happening? How can it be *real*?

"Yes," the man says.

"And you're a vampire? I mean, a real live vampire. Um, dead. A real live dead vampire. Or, um, *undead* I guess. A real undead... never mind, you know what I mean."

"How—?"

"Prove it," Mary challenges, because if she's going to go all the way crazy, she's not going without some sort of proof. She feels strongly that there ought to be scientific procedures to follow, that she should have empirical evidence before she cracks. "Do something vampiric."

Without the aid of a cut-away shot, or a team of rushed effects artists, or a directed beam of light shone through a slat taped onto a flashlight, the man's irises turn a bright, predatory yellow. He smiles and Mary actually watches as his canines slide downwards, out of the pockets in the gums in his upper jaw.

"Now," Richmond DuNoir says. He isn't even lisping. Unlike Crispin, he's had a few centuries to get used to talking around his longer teeth. "How do you know who I am?"

"I—" Mary stutters, cutting herself off with her own panic. That's all that seems to be able to come out. "I—" and, "You—" and another, "I—" Finally, she swallows and manages: "It's not possible."

"You already know my nature," Richmond says. "Can you deny now my existence?"

"No," Mary offers. "Just *mine*."

Richmond is saved from further commentary by the arrival of a nurse. Mary takes only a moment to marvel that this world actually works the way a television show does: no awkward breaks, no boring day-to-day. In one scene and out to another, from plot point to plot point, all neatly cut together. She wonders what happens when it's time for the commercial break. Do people actually pause? Will she see the ads flashing around her? Will she be a part of them?

She turns to ask as much of Richmond, but he is gone. The window is shut. The nurse flicks on the overhead light and makes a soft little exclamation of surprise and expresses her delight at seeing that the Miss Jane Doe is awake and upright. She eagerly takes up the chart hanging from the bottom of her bed, pen raised in predatory preparation.

Mary gives her information, her name and phone number and emergency contact. The nurse takes them, and her chart, and her vitals, and then leaves. Mary drinks more water and tries not to have hysterics. It's pretty easy when you're concentrating on it, the not having them part. She wonders if they'll sneak up on her eventually, when she's not paying attention. She's not sure she can focus on anything for that long, that intensely. Especially not her own sanity. That's the sort of thing that's supposed to be a given, to be automatic like breathing and blinking, and she doesn't like the idea that she's going to have to concentrate.

The doctor returns about half an hour later with his *we need to talk* face on. It seems as though there is no Mary here. Her apartment building doesn't exist, and they had even sent an orderly to drive over and check. It's a pizzeria. Her name is not in the phone book. She has no wallet. It must have fallen from her pocket when she was struck by the van. Or else, someone might have picked her pocket while she was lying by the side of the road. She's not sure which idea disturbs her more.

She doesn't have the heart to tell them to try her parents' number. She is too tired right now, too exhausted with disappointment and terror to be told that they don't exist either.

The doctor asks her name again, slow and careful, but this time, Mary assumes that he's making notes about her cognitive abilities, making suggestions on the chart clutched close to his chest for amnesia testing and psychoanalytic consultation, and perhaps multiple personality disorder as a result of the crash.

Mary almost hopes that this is the case. That her whole life up until now has been some sort of fantasy. That she really *is* crazy. Because anything else is more sane than admitting that she has fallen into a television show that she used to work on, and that in this place, she doesn't exist. Maybe this Mary died at birth. Maybe this Mary never went to film school. Maybe this Mary fell in love with Johnston Pertin from grade ten and got married and had five million kids.

Maybe this Mary never got written into existence because in TV shows, nobody needs parking PAs.

*****

The hospital has no grounds on which to hold her, even if they say that she doesn't exist. So, after a night of bed rest and another day of observation, Mary is given her clothing back and released into Night City with a bottle of pills clutched in her hand and a spectacular black and blue mottle of bruising on her left cheek and down her jaw. She is lucky, she realizes in retrospect, to still have all of her teeth. Her jeans and jacket are torn, right above the places where the stitches are. She's given instructions to drink plenty of fluids and take short naps rather than long sleeps, and have someone wake her up every hour.

Mary has no idea where to go to sleep, let alone where to find someone to wake her up. She knows no one, is known to no one. She doesn't even have her wallet with her, which means that she has no credit cards with which to get a hotel room. She only knows one person in the whole city, and he isn't even real. He's a fictional character.

All the same, she climbs into the first cab that will take her, and says, "Number five, Rose Street, please." It feels natural. As the man at the centre of this fictional universe, to whom else should she turn but him?

"Rose Street?" the cabbie asks, glancing at her bruised face, her torn clothing in the rear view mirror. "That's the old warehouse district, lady," he adds in a perfect blurt of exposition. It set's Mary's teeth on edge. *Bad writing.*

"I know," Mary says. She is too tired and too sore, and maybe too crazy to fight with anyone else today. "Please just go there."

The cabbie pulls away from the curb. At first, he tries to engage her in small talk, but she is too busy frowning at the Night City crest on his driver's permit to answer back, and he takes the hint. He drives legally, carefully, exactly like an extra ought to drive, and nothing at all like the real cabbies do. He never runs one light or hops one curb. He seems to take the most direct route, and they arrive more quickly than she expects, pausing at no stoplights. They were all green.

Richmond du Noir, like any television vampire worth his undead salt, does not live in something as urbane as a condominium. When they pull up in front of five Rose Street, the cabbie peers up dubiously at the seemingly abandoned vaudeville theatre. He glances at the meter—$25.60—then back at her. "I'll take you to the nearest subway station for free, lady," he offers.

"No. Wait here. My friend will pay you."

"Some friend, if he lives here," the cabbie says. But he waits all the same as Mary awkwardly clambers out of the back of the cab, trying not to strain her stitches. By the time she gets to the front door, Richmond DuNoir is already there.

He probably heard the car engine stopping outside of his building and came to investigate. He is leaning on the outside of the jamb, hands in his pockets, and he doesn't look surprised that it is Mary who has wriggled her aching way out of the cab and limps the few steps toward him. He is not smiling.

She stops and wonders if this was a Very Bad Idea. Well, if it is, it is also a Too Late revelation. "I have no money for the cab," Mary admits.

Richmond ushers her into the alcove of the stage door, pulls his wallet out of his jacket pocket then goes out and tosses a fifty at the cabbie. "She was never here," he says, and the cabbie nods, agreeing to the bribe, and peels away.

Mary waits for Richmond at the bottom of the stairs. Partly because she's scared of going up into the apartment set alone, and partly because she's not sure she has the strength for it. She's eaten nothing but blue Jell-O and reconstituted eggs all day, and she's still not feeling so hot from getting run over.

Oh, and the whole shifting into a fictional reality has her pretty loopy, too.

Richmond threads one cold arm around her waist for support, strong and oddly solid, and lets her pick her way up the narrow flight of stairs by herself. They both know he could just scoop her up and carry her like a doll, and she appreciates that he understands that she'd rather do it on her own. He's intuitive like that, something she'd always called a virtue in the man, but others online often called a fault in the writing; that the writers assume too much.

Richmond doesn't ask Mary any questions. He just helps her over to the red leather sofa, then strips off his jacket and throws it across the back. He goes back to his disused kitchenette and pours her a glass of water from the taps, and comes back to give it to her. She takes it, thanks him, and drinks shakily. Unsure what to do with himself, Richmond turns on his electric fireplace, then a few lamps, and circles back to double check the fireplace setting. He lives in the fly gallery of the old theatre that he used to run before moving pictures stole away most of his audience. Unsure how to keep up with this technological rival, he converted the top into an apartment for himself—luxurious bathroom, cozy bedroom, sprawling living room sprinkled with solidly built antique furniture, and a utilitarian kitchenette for the sake of appearances—and left the auditorium to rot.

That's where he met Sherri, a street kid who is actually quite pretty under the grime. Ugly people are never really ugly on television. Sherri found the abandoned theatre and started sleeping in the seats. It wasn't until she got brave enough to give in to her urge to try out the acoustics that Richmond even knew that she was there.

That was all in the pilot episode of course; it's been two years now, or maybe more? Mary wonders who is further ahead in the time line, the production or this reality? Is she destroying the hard work the writers are putting into Season Three? A sharp pang of maliciousness roars up her breastbone and she thinks: *I hope so!*

Sherri is living with the foster family that Richmond found for her, and going to school—when she isn't using her acting skills to help him trap killers or outwit monsters, of course. She dreams of being a Broadway star, and Richmond wants to help her. He has some connections, still. But Antonio, who made Richmond what he is, doesn't like that a mortal knows about their true nature. He wants Richmond to kill Sherri, or convert her. Richmond refuses to do either, to take her dream of a life on the stage away from Sherri. It is a continual tension in the series, overlaid by the weekly mystery that Richmond solves before the local constabulary does to keep them from finding out that the supernatural actually exists.

Antonio is no help; he wants nothing more than to be exposed. He wants the monsters to rule the world again, the way they used to. He hates skulking in the shadows. Sometimes, he even deliberately sabotages Richmond's attempts to keep things covered up. The Season One cliffhanger saw real evidence of vampiric existence being mailed to the hardened police chief, and Richmond scrambling against the clock and the sunrise to get it back. Richmond succeeded, of course, but it still hasn't been cleared up who actually mailed it. Mary, along with most of the fanbase, is pretty sure it was Antonio.

"Hello, there you are," Richmond says when Mary finally blinks and looks up from her empty glass. "Where did you go? Flashback or brooding?"

Mary can't help but laugh at the complete and utter earnestness with which he delivers such a clichéd line. Crispin Okafor may be bored with the role, but he still has talent. Then Mary frowns—this isn't Crispin, this is Richmond, and she will have to learn to allow herself to believe in him as a person and not a character if she's going to keep a tight grip on that oh-so-precious sanity she was contemplating earlier.

"Neither," Mary admits. "Thinking."

"About?"

"You?"

Richmond DuNoir has lost all ability to blush, but he ducks his head with a sort of boyish charm that startles Mary. She's never seen him do that on the show. This is all Richmond, no Crispin whatsoever. It really hammers home that Mary is not where she should be, that she is lost here, now, alone and with no idea whether she's gone nuts, or is in a coma, or if this has really happened.

This isn't fiction, it's real. She is breathing the air, she can feel the sofa below her, taste the staleness of Richmond's tap water, the dust on the glasses. Out the window, the city shines, mobile and real, and not at all a matte painting. Richmond isn't a construct of dialogue and lighting, but a person. A real living, breathing (in a manner of speaking) person.

She sets down the glass on the Italianate coffee table in front of her before it can shake right out of her fingers.

"Are you okay, Miss?" Richmond asks again and seems torn between sitting down beside her and staying as far away as possible. He can't seem to intuit what she wants this time, and that's no surprise. Mary is not even sure herself. She burns to touch him, to feel the silk of his shirt between her fingers, to run her hands down his jaw and the perpetual five o'clock shadow that he will not ever be able to shave away; but she is equally desperate to get away, to run screaming from this person who *cannot be*.

She wants it to be real and is too frightened of what it may mean if it is.

"I'm tired," she finally admits. "Sore. I was hit by a car."

"Right." Richmond snaps his fingers, as if he'd forgotten. "Do you have pain medication?"

Mary digs the little orange bottle out of her coat pocket. Richmond whisks away her glass again, off to the tap and eager to be a good host. Mary struggles out of her ruined jacket and lays it over the arm of the sofa next to Richmond's. It looks so cheap next to his, even though they're the same cut, the same color. His is real leather, and hers is just a knock off of Richmond's. Mary feels her cheeks go all hot with embarrassment.

Richmond comes back and by the way his eyes narrow, she can tell that he is watching the way her blood moves under her skin. She'd seen that look before, which makes her blush more, forehead and cheeks burning. Richmond swallows hard, suddenly blinking as if he just realized what he was doing.

"I have no food," Richmond says, by way of apology for staring. He puts the glass back into Mary's hand, shakes two pills out of the bottle into her palm, and watches carefully as she takes both. "I could order a pizza? I think?"

"I'm not hungry," Mary admits. "Go ahead if you are."

Then she stops and wishes desperately that the ground would open up and swallow her whole. What a horribly callous thing to say!

She meant to be polite, a good guest, but forgot that she was the guest of a vampire. And Richmond DuNoir does not drink the blood of human beings anymore.

"Sorry!" she says immediately, before the shocked look can properly crawl across Richmond's face. "I forgot that you...you're a...I didn't mean it like that!" She's not entirely sure how he *thinks* she meant it. His eyes flick once to her neck, then away. He turns on his heel, goes to his refrigerator and pulls out a bottle. He pours himself a champagne flute full, and it is thick and red. He drinks the whole glass, clinging to the stem as if it could ward off whatever it was that was lurking in his gaze as he watches her. Then he pours himself a second, puts the bottle back, and returns to the living room.

He sits down on the armchair beside the sofa, also red leather, and says, "It doesn't bother you?" He lifts the glass slightly to indicate what he's talking about.

"Why should it?" Mary asks. "I know what you are."

"Yes, about that," Richmond says and sets down the glass of blood beside her empty water glass. "How?"

"It's not Sherri," Mary says hastily. "She'd never."

His frown gets deeper. "*Miss*...?" he says.

"Mary," Mary corrects. "You can... can call me Mary. Richmond."

He blinks. "Mary. Yes. *How?*"

Mary sighs. The painkillers are kicking in and she can already feel herself starting to drift off. She thinks

35

she should be more concerned about falling asleep in the presence of a vampire, especially since she's already insinuated that he's allowed to drink her blood.

But this is Richmond DuNoir, and Mary knows him. Mary *trusts* him. Mary might even love him a little bit.

"You'd never believe me," she says.

If Richmond answered, Mary's asleep before she can hear it.

She's never fallen asleep so fast from painkillers, but it's a convenient way to insert an act break, so she doesn't try to fight it.

Chapter Three :
Villains are Only Sexy
on the Other Side of the Screen

The one thing Mary has forgotten—or maybe the one thing that she's never bothered to remember—is that vampires are, ultimately, monsters.

Hungry, powerful, scary monsters.

When she wakes to find Antonio standing in Richmond's living room, glaring down at her, she is very immediately reminded. For the first time in her life, Mary feels like prey. Something small and old deep in the back of her brain recalls what it's like to be at the bottom of the food chain, to be hunted by things with sharper teeth, sharper senses, and sharper claws.

Antonio is a glorious Italian monster, with long dark

hair, thick dark lashes, and dusky dark skin. The actor, Larry Byrne, was born in Vancouver and has to take weekly accent lessons. He goes tanning a lot, and wears falsies on set.

Before Mary can even register enough to take a breath to scream, Richmond is launching himself at Antonio with a dramatic, "No!"

Antonio ducks out of the way and lets Richmond's own momentum carry him into the stone wall opposite. Mary winces as Richmond ricochets and hits the ground hard.

"What is this, Richmon?" Antonio asks, rolling the "r" of Richmond's name in a sinister, delicious way that makes Mary shiver. His black eyes pin her to the sofa. "Another urchin? How many do you plan on adopting, Richmon? Or have you finally come to your senses and this one is for me?"

"Don't touch her!" Richmond screams from the floor, and Mary wonders why he doesn't just stand up and wallop Antonio back. Yes, moaning from the floor is nice and dramatic for a plot line, but this is Mary's life here! The hero can get up and start saving it any second now!

There's no reason not to. Oh, unless she's been cast as the starlet of the week? They die a lot. Mary doesn't like that thought, so she deliberately stops thinking it. Instead, she starts thinking about how to escape.

"Leave her alone!" Richmond howls.

Antonio, of course, does the exact opposite of what Richmond wants, he always has, and leans right down into Mary's personal space, arms folded thoughtfully behind his back, hair a black sheet, cascading off his shoulders as he gets closer. Mary shrinks back against the arm of the sofa and wonders why on Earth she ever thought Antonio in person would be sexy.

He's not sexy, he's freaking terrifying!

There's something about him, the dark masculine alpha dog *menace* that he exudes like a miasma, the preciseness of his almost clockwork-like movements, which are all that break up his deathly stillness. Richmond, at least, feels like he *used* to be human—but Antonio doesn't feel like anything but a creature, a *thing*. It's cloying and heavy and it just doesn't bleed through the television screen. His mere presence presses down on her, and she wishes there was a screen between them now.

Antonio is a fiend. Antonio was a fiend before he ever died.

He did things...he was a celebrated soldier and a selfish politician, yes, one of the most famous lovers of all time... but generous, kind, and considerate? Pretty much the opposite. Antonio has never hesitated when it comes to taking what—or who—he wants. He has always liked the fighters, the screamers...the ones who cry, "No." It's more fun when they break.

The overwhelming *presence* of Antonio makes Mary want to scream. It makes her want to roll over and expose her belly like a submissive puppy in the hopes that pleasing him will grant her mercy. It makes her want to curl up and cry.

Mary takes a deep breath, screws up her courage. She dredges up what little alpha-ness she has of her own, and clutches it tight.

"Erm," Mary says. Antonio doesn't move back, doesn't stop the slow invasion into her personal bubble, just plants his hands on either side of her shoulders and nudges his nose up under the curve of her jaw. His breath is freezing against her skin, and she feels every pore contract in horror. "Signor Antonio..."

He hums once against the underside of her ear, and she takes this as indication that he's listening.

"Uh," she says. "Um, please don't eat me."

Antonio barks a laugh into her ear so loud that she wants to clap her hands over them, but can't, because his hands are now holding her by the elbows. It hurts. The scrapes, the stitches, and the asphalt burn there, and Mary hisses to keep from whimpering. She wriggles, trying to get her feet under her, trying to get enough leverage to kick him.

"I like this one, Richmon," Antonio says, pulling back to look into Mary's eyes. His own are glowing a dangerous yellow, and Mary swallows hard on the scream trying to claw up her throat. Antonio likes screamers, and she won't give him the pleasure. "Maybe not for killing, then? Did you bring for me a little treat?"

"No!" Richmond says again, and Mary is starting to get very, very annoyed with his impotent lying around. *Anytime now, Richy-boy*, she thinks. *You've got the fireplace poker right freakin' there!*

But the vampires in this reality cannot read minds. Antonio slides his hands down Mary's arms, crushing her wrists together in one hand before using the other to grab her chin and force her to look straight into his gaze.

"No you don't," Mary says, and squeezes her eyes shut. She isn't about to be just one more in a long line of stupid guest star girls-of-the-week who get ensnared by Antonio's python gaze.

Antonio chuckles again, and this time, Mary does let forth a little terrified mewl. Richmond is still being entirely useless, screaming, "No, please, no," from the other side of the coffee table, but still too much of a coward to actually hit the man who made him undead, even to save Mary's life.

It's not his fault, though, Mary forgives him. It's just the way he was written.

She's going to have to save herself.

Mary wriggles her hands and Antonio lets go, sliding his other hand up her stomach, across her breast—ew!—and up her throat to tangle in her hair and wrench her head to the side. It hurts, hot pulling blazing up from her shoulder blade along her shoulder and to the base of her skull. He's probably torn something, some muscle she doesn't remember the name of. But she doesn't have the time to care now because her hands are free.

Mary can feel his fangs skittering over the skin above her jugular, a teasing scrape that makes her want to go still in the absurd rabbit-like wish that he'll mistake her for dead and go away. She can't, though, not if she wants him off her.

She hears the telltale hiss that means Antonio is about to strike and flails out. She kicks at his kneecap, using her heel to crack against the side. Antonio howls and jerks back, stumbling. Mary scrambles around him and dives

41

toward the kitchen. She runs to the most logical place for a utensil drawer to be, but there is nothing in it. Nor is there in any of the other drawers and she wastes precious seconds searching the counter for a knife block. Nothing. Everything is empty. No weapons. Not even a frying pan.

"Oh, are you goddamn kidding me?" she hisses to herself. "Right, why *would* a vampire have a cooking knife?"

Strong fingers grab the back of her neck. She is yanked backward, losing her footing, slamming into something so solid that her stomach is driven up against her spine. Antonio slides one arm down from her shoulders along her body, pulling her arms together in front of her, crushing her wrists in a one-handed grip. He leans down and brushes his fangs against her neck.

Mary kicks back and nails Antonio right in the nuts. He howls and jerks back. She reaches up and pulls down a wine glass from an open cupboard. She swings it hard, twisting around, eyes closed. The glass smashes against Antonio. She hopes it was his goddamn face. He snarls and lets go again. She turns and opens her eyes. The stem of the wine glass is sticking out of Antonio's ear canal, his flesh peppered with shards of glass.

Ew.

Antonio touches his face. His fingers come away bloody, and he stares in amazement at the mess. Mary scrambles over to the fireplace while he is distracted, trying to get Richmond between them. There is a wrought iron sweep set by the hearth, and she seizes on that, lifting up the poker threateningly. Richmond, great useless anti-hero that he is, stands there and stares in gob-smacked amazement.

Someone has actually fought back against Antonio, wonder of wonders.

Richmond seems to finally get a clue and grabs a weapon, too, hefting the dustpan like a sword, with a determined look on his face

"Hello, finally!" Mary snaps at him.

The sound of her voice attracts Antonio's attention. He whips around and snarls at them, then stops in confusion when he sees that they're both wielding wrought iron weapons. He does not seem concerned about Mary's poker, but he takes a second look at the ash pan. He touches the glass sticking out of his face gingerly. Then he licks his own blood off his fingertips, his expression thoughtful.

"I am so disappointed, Richmon." He sighs dramatically. "You used to be such an obedient boy. She's a bad influence."

"Fuck off," Mary spits. She's not sure who's most surprised by her pronouncement: Antonio, for having such profanities directed at him, or Richmond for her daring, or Mary, for having enough idiotic courage to actually say it. "Fuck off!" she says again, because it feels good, *damn* good! Why has she been so careful with her cusses before? This feels *great*. Possibly, it could be the fault of the drugs or the adrenaline. "Fuck off, fuck off, fuck off! Leave me alone, and leave Richmond alone. Go away! Forever!"

"You cannot order me!" Antonio thunders, drawing himself upright. He looks ridiculous with the bottom half a wine glass sticking out of the side of his head like a Halloween party favor.

"Well, I am," Mary says. "Go away and never come back. Richmond isn't yours anymore."

Antonio grins. "Oh, isn't he? I made him what he is. He is my child. And you, you impertinent little thing, you will feel my fangs in your throat soon enough!"

That has got to be the most clichéd thing she had ever heard him say, but Mary knows an Antonio exit speech when she hears one, and isn't at all surprised when he suddenly vanishes from her sight.

If he's stayed true to the show, and there's no reason to assume he hasn't, he's gone back to his underground crypt to lick his wounds—well, to have one of his perverted subordinates pick out all the glass and lick them, at any rate. She and Richmond will be okay for the rest of the night, at least. Antonio never attacks twice in twenty-four hours. He thinks it's gauche.

Weary, Mary drops the fireplace poker on the floor and shuffles over to the other side of the sofa, where the floor isn't covered with glass shards and flecks of blood. Richmond stays where he is, his hands shaking so badly that the pan is actually rattling.

"Richmond?" she asks.

"You...you told him to go," Richmond whispers, awed. "And he *went*."

"He's a manipulative masochistic bastard who only likes to play for as long as his prey is under his control. Show an ounce of self-determination and he flees. Didn't you know that?"

Richmond shakes his head, paler than normal, which turns him a sickly sort of bronze, dark eyes wide, and Mary feels a sudden pity for him. He was written to be earnest, naive, sweet. A nice man thrust into a terrible situation. It's not his fault he's sort of clueless.

"Come here," Mary says, and she stands and limps over to him. She wraps her arms around his waist, rests her head on his chest, and squeezes as much as the stitches allow.

At first, Richmond doesn't move, statuary-still in his obvious shock. Then he drops the pan, wraps his arms around her shoulders and very carefully hugs back. He rests his cheek against the top of her head, whispers, "Mary" and, "thank you" and, "oh, God" over and over and over again.

Mary thinks she should be surprised when he nudges her forehead back with his nose, when he dips in low for a sweet and lingering kiss. She isn't of course, because she's watched almost every episode of *City by Night*, and she knows that the only way that Richmond understands how to show his gratitude is by bringing joy and bliss to others. Usually in the form of orgasms. Nakedness is good for ratings.

She lets him wrap his hands around her ass, lets him lift her up against him to straddle his waist and just concentrates on kissing open his mouth, on letting his tongue tease in between her lips, on learning the feel of his fangs carefully with the tip of her own tongue.

He walks them toward the bedroom and Mary thinks, *I'm going to have hot kinky bloodplay sex with Richmond DuNoir! Fantastic!*

Richmond is a very deft hand at buttons and zippers and is very careful of her stitches and bruises and cuts. He kisses each hurt gently, carefully, making his way down one side of her body and up the other. Mary lets him turn her over, nip at the back of her knees, at the curve of her hip, the swell of her lower back.

She wants to touch him, but he pushes her hands up above her head, and she's happy to leave them there, to grab at the headboard, and let him do whatever he wants. Richmond has never liked being touched. He strips himself and nestles between her legs. She's never seen his penis on TV, of course, and is both slightly thrilled at the sight of it, the juxtaposition of that dark skin resting on her own thigh, and slightly disappointed that it's still flaccid.

"I need blood first," he pants against her neck, following her gaze. "Please, Mary."

"Yes," she says, and another shiver of anticipation, of fangirly joy marches up her body, across all her sensitive places, leaving goose bumps in its wake. "God, please, Richmond, *yes*."

Having one's blood sucked is not quite as sensual as Mary expected. It hurts, for one thing, the hard drive of teeth through the hyper-sensitized flesh of her neck. And when he begins to suck, it doesn't feel anything at all like an impending orgasm or the best chocolate ever, or any of the other metaphors and allusions the show uses. Or the fan fiction, for that matter.

It just feels like someone is sucking her blood out of her neck.

Uncomfortable and very, very weird.

But then, Richmond drops his hand down between them and Mary feels the unmistakable brush of hard flesh against her entrance, and the blood sucking doesn't matter anymore, because Richmond is very, very good at this part all on its own.

*****

Sometime later, when the sun has risen and they've tired themselves out, Richmond rolls over in his sleep and pulls Mary tight against him like a teddy bear. The position scratches her stitches along his hard stomach, and she jerks awake at the jolt of pain. She takes a millisecond to revel. This, this is all real, this has all happened, and she is here. *Here.* In this world. In this bed.

Then Mary gasps, says "ouch" and tries to wriggle out of his grip. Richmond is very strong, and she can't break his hold.

She can, however, turn over within the circle of his arms, and she wriggles some more until she's face to face. She says, "Richmond. Richmond, wake up. Sleeping Beauty. Hey! Yo! *Wake up!*" But he doesn't.

She bites the end of his nose.

That works. "Mary?" He is bleary and glassy eyed. "Did you just bite my nose?"

"Yes."

"How adorably domestic."

"Yeah, I guess, but...uhg, let go, you're hurting me."

Richmond comes all the way awake and somehow spreads himself out like a starfish above Mary, a funny man-shaped tent.

"Hi," she says.

"Hi," he says back. He is smiling. "Good morning."

"You look ridiculous."

He grins harder and lowers himself enough that they're pressed together from nose to kneecap. "Better?"

"Yes."

He dips his head for a kiss that Mary is more than willing to give up. "You're amazing," he says.

Mary fights the urge to blush. She's not sure she has enough blood left for it, anyway. Her stomach gives a little grumble, and they both laugh. Richmond reaches across the bed for the telephone on his side table and orders a large cheese pizza from a place on the other end of town.

"There, thirty minutes to ourselves," he says. "Me and my amazing Mary."

"Stop calling me amazing," Mary protests.

"You beat off Antonio. You made him run away. That's amazing in my book."

Mary feels instantly annoyed, all the arousal and affection draining away in her irritation. "For God's sake, Richmond," she says. "You're more than capable of doing it, too."

"But Antonio is...he's my...my Maker, I can't."

And there it is, the one niggling piece of logic in the whole show that Mary has not been able to swallow. "Yeah, now, see, I don't actually get that. I never have. Why not?" she asks. "It's not as if you owe him your loyalty, and he certainly hasn't earned it."

Richmond doesn't seem to understand. "But he's..."

"He hurt you! He still hurts you, all the time. He's *mean* to you."

"He means well," Richmond says, but even he doesn't seem convinced.

"But he doesn't!" Mary insists. "He doesn't! You don't owe him anything!"

"He made me..."

"Against your express permission! He's a colonialist bastard! Richmond, it was..." She hates the word, hates to say it out loud, has always hated it even before it became terrifyingly relevant and real to her in Antonio's embrace. "It was rape."

Richmond looks like he's seriously never contemplated it before. "Rape?"

Very carefully, she touches his cheek with her palm. It's room temperature, not at all as cold as it was a few hours ago, before they curled up into his bed to cuddle like a pair of teenagers. Mary seriously underestimated the simple happiness that cuddling can bring. "He asked for...for you to do something intimate with him," Mary whispers. "And you said no."

She waits for realization to dawn on Richmond's face, but this is television and pretty obvious television at that, so sometimes characters need things spelled out for them. It's not that Richmond is inherently stupid, just that he's been written to need the lines drawn between A and B and C for him.

"You said, no." Mary pushes as he flounders in silence, waiting for the next connection. "And he did it anyway. Pretty much fits the definition."

Richmond frowns. His eyebrows dip into that dangerous vee that Mary knows so well from the posters and promotional shots, the concerned thinky-face that is endearing and makes her heart flutter whenever she sees it.

He's flashbacking.

Mary waits for the world around her to dissolve, for the universe to suddenly become a great dusty savannah, three hundred years ago. It doesn't. It stays right as it is, paused, waiting. It's not the world, but Richmond who sort of...goes.

But up close, there's an undercurrent of intensity, too, a sort of bottled rage that is almost overwhelmingly tangible. Mary is torn between wanting to squirm away in case he does let the rage go, and staying very, very still under him, like a squirrel caught in the gaze of a wolf.

She keeps forgetting that Richmond isn't human. It's a silly thing to do after Antonio's visit just last night. Also, when she has spent the last two years watching a television show about how he *isn't*. But Richmond is human-shaped and human-looking, mostly. He communicates and gestures and moves like a human most of the time, and so Mary looks at him and thinks, "human". No, she looks at him and thinks "Richmond". She doesn't even think "human" or "vampire" or even "Crispin" much after the last few hours.

Then he does something like this. He goes statue still and stops breathing and his eyes flare intense yellow, and she remembers and wonders how she ever forgets.

It's *scary*.

He isn't looking at her, she knows that. He's looking at something in his memory, something long ago, something that hurt him. He's curling up his fingers into fists, like he could strike out at the memory of what Antonio did to him. Only his hands are on her shoulders now and it *hurts*. Mary bites on her lower lip to keep from making some sort of wounded prey sound.

Richmond is heavy—Mary realizes this when all of his weight drops onto her pelvis. He was holding himself off her before, with his knees, with tensed thighs, with his elbows. He was letting her feel just enough of him to be comforting and sheltering and there. But he's strong, which means there's a lot of dense, supernatural muscle packed onto his misleadingly wiry frame, and it's all sitting right on Mary's hips.

She fists her own hands into the blankets beside his knees to keep from squirming.

Then his fingernails cut through her skin, and she can't hold back the pained keen any more, letting it bubble out as a terrified whimper. Either the scent of fresh blood or the terrified sound makes Richmond's lip curl, and his eyes hone straight in on her shoulder. For a horrifying, heart-stopping second, Richmond does not look like himself, he does not look like he recognizes Mary at all. All he probably sees is a warm body pinned beneath his own, and hot blood ready and available.

He grins, lifts one hand and licks delicately at the blood under his fingernails. His mouth slides down, over her breast, and his hand pushes down between their bodies.

Mary is scared. "Richmond!" she gasps finally, and that's it, that's enough to snap him out of his monstrous haze.

He blinks, sniffs the air and groans, but it's not a sexy sound. It is self-depreciating, self-loathing.

"God, Mary," he starts.

But she interrupts with, "Air!" Richmond lifts himself off her so quickly that he practically takes flight.

"Mary, I'm *sorry*." His voice is broken, pleading for forgiveness. Mary has heard this tone before, too, the desperate self-hatred that she always thought was too much for the character. The problem with Crispin's portrayal, she sometimes allowed herself to think, is that it was too polar; Richmond swings from one extreme of emotion to another and never seems to be able to find a way to inhabit the center.

That's what Mary's going to do. She decides it suddenly, totally. No, it's perfect, really. It makes complete sense. It explains why she's even here at all.

She sits up and gasps in breath. She turns, dangling her feet off the edge of the bed. Her toes skim the cold concrete floor, and she wishes Richmond had enough foresight to buy a rug for his human friends. She wonders if it was a deliberate choice on the part of the set decorator, an attempt to make him more inhuman, or if it was the restrictions of budget, or just sheer laziness. Either way, if she's really here, in this place, and she's really going to have to live in this world, then she's going to convince him to buy some damned throw rugs. And then she's going to convince Richmond to stop being such a drama queen and start living his life on an even keel.

And the first thing she's going to do is get him to understand that he doesn't owe Antonio a goddamned thing. So she says just that. "You don't owe Antonio a goddamned thing."

She feels Richmond drop into place beside her, his cool arm going around her waist. She wonders if he's struggling between paying attention to her admonishments and watching her bleed.

"Mary," he whines again, drawing out her name like an impatient two-year-old.

"Oh, go ahead," she says, lifting her shoulders in a subtle shrug. His tongue is moist and cold against her skin, like being licked by an ice cube, and she shivers. Richmond is breathing hard through his nose, making heavy gasping sounds as though he's about three seconds away from an orgasm. Mary shivers when she realizes that it's not because he's breathing, but because he's *smelling*. The air he puffs out against the small hairs at the nape of her neck is hot, hot now, and she closes her eyes, lets her head rest on his arm as he licks and licks and licks.

He has the self-restraint to stop once the bleeding has. Mary feels more than a little flushed and a lot distracted. Her body complains that it hasn't finished what was started, but she forces herself to open her eyes, to sit up again, to remember what it was that she was going to say.

"Richmond," she says.

"I'm sorry," he says again. Miserable.

"Don't be sorry for being what you are. I *like* it," Mary snaps and there, she's said it. Richmond looks up, startled, and she twists sideways and grabs his hands. Like a necklace just put on, she can feel the warmth from her skin sinking into his, heating him up with her own warmth. "Antonio—"

Richmond looks down at his feet.

Mary grabs his chin and turns his face back up so she can meet his eyes. They're brown again, and they look like they ought to be in the face of a beagle puppy that's just been kicked.

"Now, you listen to me, Richmond DuNoir!" she shouts. "Antonio raped you! And you hate it, and that's good! You should! He raped you, and he locked you up in his big fancy villa with a bunch of other people who said 'yes' in order to force you to be grateful. They brainwashed you into feeling like you owe him something, but you *don't*! Antonio kidnapped and killed you, and that's not love, that's not loyalty, that's *sick*. And he's made you sick."

"Mary," Richmond gasps, but Mary talks over him.

"That's fucking Stockholm Syndrome, that's what it is!"

Richmond is suddenly gone.

Mary's hands are empty, and she's shouting at thin air, at the early dawn rays that are coming into the room in glowing shafts, cut up by the cheap mini-blinds.

"Well, shit," Mary says, and lies back down and clutches at Richmond's pillow and closes her eyes. "Drama queen."

She does not sleep.

Chapter Four :
Exactly as Expected and Entirely Overrated

Mary answers the door wearing Richmond's dressing gown, and pays the pizza delivery guy with money that she finds in his wallet, which was in the leather jacket hanging on the hall tree by the door. She doesn't count the number of bills in there, but it's a lot. She's never seen anyone dumb enough to carry that much cash at once, but then it's not like anyone would dare try to pickpocket Richmond. And if they did succeed, they wouldn't get to hold on to it for long, that's for sure.

She's not hungry anymore, so she drops the steaming pizza box onto the coffee table, walks around the broken glass, and goes into the washroom. She pokes through

Richmond's medicine cabinet— devoid of anything except a toothbrush, toothpaste, mouthwash, hair gel, and a comb—and it doesn't make her feel better. There are no great secrets there, no deep understanding of her personality on offer. The fangirly glee is gone, washed away in the melancholy revelation that these people are actually real, and that they actually do believe what they've been written to believe.

It is maddening. Everything she likes about the world of *City by Night* when it is on TV is, in reality, annoying, incomprehensible, illogical, vapid, or dangerous. Vampirism isn't sexy. It is frightening. Even Richmond isn't what she thought he was; he is just some sort of puppet that Antonio tortures, he has no spine of his own, no guts.

This isn't fun. Mary wants to go home. But she has no idea how. She doesn't have the faintest idea where to start. All her love of urban fantasy novels, of fan fiction, of comics and movies and romance books, none of it has prepared her for actually living in it ... or given her any clue how to get back out again. She doesn't know any magical rituals or mad scientists or anyone who can work real magic in this world. She doesn't even have the faintest idea where to *start*.

So what can she do, except take each moment as it comes? Stay with Richmond and heal and ... wait. To work with him, on him, and just ... wait. To wake up. For it to be over. For something. But what, she has no idea.

She drops the dressing gown onto the floor, steps into the shower and tries to use the hot water to soothe away her disappointment. The bathroom door opens and closes quietly and then Richmond is in the shower with her, wrapping his arms around her waist, burying his face in the wet hair and the nape of her neck.

"I'll try," he promises. "I'll do my best. I won't play Antonio's games anymore."

Mary doesn't say that she doesn't believe that he'll change, doesn't believe that he is *capable* of change. He's a fictional character, and he can only behave the way he's written. All the same, she lays her arms against his, cups his hands in hers, and nods.

She tries not to marvel at how quickly the cynicism has crept up.

✱✱✱✱✱

Mary eats half of the cold pizza when they get out of the shower and spends the rest of the day in Richmond's dressing gown, wondering what she's going to do for clothes, or money, or a living. Reality has hit her hard for the first time in the one place that she thought it wouldn't be able to get to her. She can't sponge off of Richmond until she dies, but she can't imagine going out into the big wide world of fictional people with their fictional dramas and to look for a fictional job. It would be like standing on the street with a neon arrow pointed at her throat and a sign that reads: "Teeth go here, Antonio!"

Richmond is in his bedroom getting dressed, and Mary wonders how Sherri deals with it. With the stress of knowing that any minute now, any night, this could be the one where Antonio breaks into the room in a shower of broken glass and splintered wood and gives her the bite. Only of course, it would never happen to Sherri, at least not until she's mature enough to deal with being undead, because this is a TV show and Sherri is played by a regular paid actor with her name in the credits. Sherri the character would never actually die. Mary doesn't feel so good about her own chances when she thinks about that.

She searches for a kettle, and a teacup, and finds them both under the sink. What she does not find is anything to make in them. Richmond, for reasons that Mary absolutely cannot fathom, keeps sherry, wine—red and white—and port in his apartment, but no tea, coffee, or soda. Typical melodramatic vampire set dressing and nothing Mary should be drinking. She's still on medication for her concussion and for the pain of her closing scars. In a few weeks, she can go back to the hospital and have the stitches removed, the doctors said. Then she'll drink Richmond's sherry, wine, and port because she'll be off the painkillers. And she'll drink until she's drunk, because frankly, she thinks she deserves it.

Between Richmond, Antonio, this world, the Craft Services van, and Mr. Geary, she feels like her eyes have been opened enough, and her self- understanding challenged to the point that alcohol- fuelled oblivion sounds absolutely awesome.

Until then, she has more water and puts the leftover pizza into the fridge, box and all, because Richmond has no cellophane wrap (why would he?) and takes another pain pill. She resists the urge to scratch at her stitches, but does poke at her asphalt burns. Richmond had peeled away the soggy bandages in the shower, mouthed each sore red patch in turn, moaning against her damp skin. She hadn't thought it that much of a turn on, but apparently he had, and there'd been enough blood in his body from earlier to show it. That had made for an interesting time in the steam.

Mary touches the side of her neck, the two small incisions, and then the descript fingernail marks, little half-moons sprinkling her shoulders. She feels smug.

Oh, if the people on her fan fiction community boards could see her now.

Mary had always thought of original characters in fan fiction as chain link fences, keeping the reader away from their desired character, but letting them see him all the same. They had always bugged her. It was voyeuristic and selfish. But now that she's on the inside of the fence, she doesn't mind half so much.

She sits on the red leather sofa, the side away from the glass, and battles with the remotes until she figures out which one turns on the television. She channel surfs and secretly hopes she finds a television program about a parking PA who gets abused horribly by her bosses. There isn't one. Mary gets annoyed, and then annoyed at herself for being annoyed at the TV, so she turns it off and goes and finds a dustpan and a broom to clean up.

Richmond comes back downstairs after the glass is tidied away (of course, men!), which luckily coincides with the sun setting. Another one of those universal synergy moments, Mary thinks. They're getting predictable.

"Are you hungry, Mary?" he asks. He does something

to her name, something with the vowel that makes her all warm and gooey inside, makes her forget her annoyance with him and this world for a little while.

"Yes," she admits. "For something other than pizza. And I want vitamins."

He frowns. "Vitamins?" Mary grins, the dirtiest most salacious grin she has. It's never worked before, not in the bars, or at the staff parties, or at conventions. But Richmond's eyes go round, and he licks his lips, and it is completely gratifying. If he was breathing, he might have been panting.

"Iron supplements," she explains, and Richmond shivers once, all over.

"Amazing woman," Richmond says, and then he's kissing her. Between the lips and the hot breath and the moist tongue, he asks, "Who are you? How do you know all these things about me? How can you be so perfect for me? It's like you were ... written in the stars. Created to be mine."

Mary doesn't answer. She smiles and turns up her face for his awe- filled kiss and lets the warm contentment growing in her belly spread to all her limbs. Sure, some moments of reality in this world are annoying, but then the moments like *this* one happen, and it makes it all worthwhile. She's enjoying this too much, even with the pain of her cuts and the fear of Antonio hanging over her head, she has Richmond, and he wants her, and that's all she's ever really wished for from life.

Really.

*****

Mary borrows some women's clothing from Richmond's closet. He can't explain why he has it, only that he does, and always has— it's weird to him that she thinks it's weird, so she drops it. Mary accepts it for the plot hole it is and doesn't question. If this little misstep in logic didn't occur, she would be going out in torn pants. Or naked.

They decide to go out for French after a stop at a very convenient all- night drug store. The drugstores are never open all night where Mary lives, but this is a television show about a vampire anti- hero, so some places have to stay open all night at least for the sake of having a variance of shooting locations.

Richmond explains, as Mary peruses the supplements bottles, that he stopped an armed robbery in here once. She knows and says as much, and he calls her amazing again and kisses her, right there under the sickly fluorescent lights that make him look more like a corpse than usual.

When they get back to his sleek car—because all the television vampires have sleek, cool cars; they have certainly had enough time to accumulate the wealth to afford them—she takes three of the iron pills dry and asks him why he thinks she's amazing. Richmond hesitates, concentrating on his driving as he gets them out onto the road from the parking lot, then says, "Because you know everything and you ... don't care. You like Richmond, me, not the vampire. Not the things I can do or will do or did do. You know everything," he says, shooting her soulful eyes. "And you love me anyway."

Mary thinks "love" is a bit of a strong verb for a feeling for a man she's only known one a day, and toward a fictional character besides. Then she reconsiders. She works to bring him to life, she faithfully watches every episode and updates the Wikipedia article page and reads his fan fiction. She attends the conventions and creates meaningful works of art centered on him. She thinks about and analyzes his motivations and gestures and verbal tics. She knows what he is, knows his flaws, knows the evil he's done, knows his unfathomable regret, and that makes him more special to her, not less.

Love is exactly what it is. When they reach the restaurant, Mary recognizes it as the one from the fifth episode of the first season, where Richmond had to pretend to be in the Mafia in order to exorcise the ghost of a miserable head chef who was murdered there by his jealous sous chef. Richmond, though he doesn't eat, somehow has a table reserved for him every night, and they sit there, right in the corner of the room with the best view across the quay to the river. They've never defined which river exactly it is that Night City is situated on, and when Mary asks, Richmond just frowns and says, "The River. That's its name."

"Oh," Mary says and feels like a fool. Of *course* that's its name. She's really starting to get the idea that this show isn't quite as well constructed as she had always tricked herself into believing it was.Mary manages to stop Richmond before he can be gracious and gallant and order a very expensive bottle of wine that neither of them can drink, and makes do with a soda and some garlic bread; light on the garlic. She orders Caesar salad and is unsure what to have for an entree because everything on the menu is so *French*. Snails and frog's legs and a million other things that some properties master must have copied off of a website titled "Best French Foods of History". Luckily, Richmond spent most of the eighteenth century in France, so he orders something called *Navarine d'angeau* for her, which turns out, thankfully, to be a very hearty lamb stew with lots of veggies.

It isn't until she's halfway through the bowl that she realizes that Richmond is looking away from her deliberately, holding his hand under his nose in a manner that seems to suggest interest in the view of the quay.

It hits Mary that he's trying to avoid looking at her. He's not breathing. He must be trying to block out the smell of the food.

"Is this gross?" Mary asks. She's been very careful with her table manners—she always is on dates, she believes that the ability to be civil in public a very big asset in partners—but she never considered that the mere act of eating would be disgusting to a vampire. Even a vampire who used to be human. All that chewing and swallowing and digesting and excreting can't be pretty to someone whose body no longer needs to do all that.

Right, and now Mary's grossed *herself* out. The waiter notices her discomfort and takes away the bowl at her little finger flick. Richmond immediately relaxes, his shoulders ratcheting down and his breath coming out in one long sigh. He'd been holding it.

"You didn't have to do that," he says, but Mary can see how grateful he is, so she only smiles and changes the topic.

More soda comes, and then the dessert cart, which Mary chooses to skip, and they talk and talk and talk until the waiter makes eyebrows at them, and Richmond lays down another wad of American cash. Mary always wondered why he only pays in cash, then considers. It's prob- ably pretty hard to get a credit card with no birth certificate. Also, cash looks better on screen and allows the characters to pay and leave without any awkward lingering to sign the bill or counting out tips. Feeling full and affectionate and appreciated—Richmond had never ever heard of a parking PA before and is fascinated with how much work actually goes into making a television program—Mary leaves the restaurant in a wonderful mood, her arms threaded around his elbow ostensibly to help take the weight off her still aching leg, and looking forward to getting back to his theatre and a bit of privacy.

She should have known that they would get sidetracked. The scream that rents the air is absolute music to hear. This must be a really talented guest star. The scream may even be digitally augmented. Richmond perks up immediately and would have taken off to follow the sound without a sideways glance at her if Mary hadn't tightened her grip on his arm in surprise. He shoots her a bit of an apologetic, but desperate look.

She nods, not liking it, but understanding; this is what Richmond does. This is what he was created for. He drops his car keys into her outstretched hands and runs away so fast Mary barely sees the asphalt dust he's kicked up in his wake.

The slick car is rather cavernous when she's in it alone, but all the same, Mary climbs in, puts the keys in the ignition so she can turn on the radio, and locks all the doors.

She tries not to think about what Richmond may be up to, if perhaps he's in over his head this time, if maybe she should really go out there, if she's playing the kind of guest star who can help him, or the kind that will just get kidnapped or killed or turned into a zombie or something. She's in the car for about two minutes, debating if she should stay or go, when suddenly all the hairs on the back of her neck stand at attention. She glances up to the rear-view mirror. But of course, there's no reflection.

"Antonio," she says softly, and she knows she's right, because that's the way these shows play.

The slick car rocks a little bit as he shifts forward in the back seat. One long, cold finger runs up the side of her neck and curls around the lobe of her ear. Mary is too scared to try to jerk away, just goes with it as Antonio uses the grip on her ear to turn it toward his mouth.

"Hello, Mary," he whispers and his voice is like an oil slick, his breath stinks of rotting meat. He's nowhere near as conscientious of his oral hygiene as Richmond. Mary gags. "You hurt me, Mary. You hurt my face, and you hurt my pride, and worst of all, you've hurt my relationship with my boy."

"You don't have any relationship with Ricmmmmungh!" Antonio twists her ear viciously.

"Richmon is *mine*," Antonio hisses. "And that makes any play- thing of his mine, too; Mary, Mary, quite contrary."

"No," Mary whispers, arching up out of her seat to try to relieve the painful pulling on her ear.

"Yes, yes, yes," Antonio says. "And I'm going to have fun playing with you; I'm going to follow you, every night, Contrary Mary, and every time he thinks you're safe from me, I'm going to prove him wrong, just a little bit. Until he acknowledges who is more powerful, who he belongs to, who should have his loyalty. And submits."

"But he won't!" Mary snarls back, because her mouth is some- times faster than her brain, and said mouth hasn't seemed to cotton on to the fact that this is no longer an RPG or a debate in a fan forum, but real, terrifying life. She can't log out, or shut the computer, or walk away. "He never will, because he's not made that way. I'm going to make sure he never does; I'm going to give him a spine, Antonio."

The pain in her ear vanishes suddenly—Antonio is still holding on, but it doesn't hurt. Adrenaline is *awesome*. She feels great. Some- thing is swelling under her sternum, and the stitches in her arm and leg don't throb, and she feels *great*. It's that same hot flash of pride at having written scene that is good, really good, of a line that will make the fans cheer. The joy of doing something *fantastic*.

Mary's head is bouncing off the dashboard before she has time to register that Antonio pushed her. She hits it with her forehead and has a split second to be grateful that it wasn't the bridge of her nose before she feels Antonio's strong fingers tangle in her hair, pulling her back flush against the seat. She flails, heels banging in the foot wells, arms slapping against the stick shift, the roller handle that controls the window.

This is not a script. This *hurts*. All the happy pride drains away into racing, darting fear.

She flings out her left arm and slams her fist into the center of the steering wheel, making the car's horn shriek with urgency, but nobody comes running out of the restaurant. Richmond does not come flying round the corner. The night stays conveniently empty. "See?" Antonio chuckles, his fetid breath skimming over her cheeks into her ear. He follows that breath with his tongue. Mary tries to cringe away, but his arm is through the hole in the headrest gripping her hair in a tight fist, unyielding.

"Let me go," she whispers into the rush of silence that follows the horn's blast.

"No," Antonio whispers back, and snuffles his face up under her jaw, nipping at the scabs that Richmond left behind that morning. "That, my Contrary Mary, is never going to happen."

Chapter Five :
Being Stuck in Bed is Only Fun When There are Handcuffs

When Mary wakes up again—and she's starting to get really sick of being knocked out, really, the writers need to come up with a better way to cut to a commercial—she is back in Richmond's bed and floating in a haze of pain. She feels cotton mouthed and shaky and her neck aches something fierce. *From the ear tugging, or the biting?* She wonders and decides not to choose between them. There is a glass of water on the bedside table, her orange bottle of pain pills right beside it.

Hands, not Antonio's and not Richmond's, help her sit up and take a pill with the water. When Mary looks up to thank her benefactor, she blinks. The girl is outlined by the full blaze of the afternoon sun coming in through the slatted blinds, her face obscured in harsh shadow, but Mary would know her anywhere.

This is Sherri, the show's third character, the spunky street urchin with the daddy- complex and eyes far too old for her face. Mary always secretly thought that this probably was the result of having a teenager playing a thirteen- year- old, but had never said so. Besides, here, right now, this Sherri *is* thirteen.

"Hello, Sherri," Mary croaks and gratefully accepts another sip of water.

"Hm," Sherri says, tilting her head to the side in that way that means she's trying to figure something out. "He said that you knew a creepy amount about us."

It's an opening for exposition, and a rather clumsy one at that, Mary thinks.

"I've only just met you and we're going to fail the Bechdel Test in our first conversation, aren't we?"

Sherri just looks at her strangely. "Bechdel Test?"

"Where two named female characters in a show have a conversation about anything except men?"

"Is that important?"

Mary sighs, not in the mood to explain herself just now. "Appar-ently not."

Sherri doesn't seem to be in the mood to hear it, either. She keeps talking as if she had never been interrupted. "You're lucky," Sherri says. She leans across Mary to put the glass of water down, and Mary can see the flash of the overlapping vampire bite scars on her neck that the effects makeup artists sometimes forget to paint on. "Antonio doesn't often leave people alive. Richmond thinks it's a message. So do I."

"So we're talking about *two* men instead?" Mary scoffs. "No, no, never mind. It is. A message, I mean. It's Antonio. It can't be anything else. He loves this cryptic mess- with- your- head crap."

"Hm," says Sherri again. Sherri makes a lot of noncommittal sounds. Mary has heard the director complain about it—the actress isn't very good at memorizing her lines and sometimes needs a moment to think about them beforehand. "I'm going to order a pizza. What do you want?

"There's half a cheese one downstairs." Sherri wrinkles her nose cutely. "I don't like leftovers. Richmond left me some money and told me to get whatever you wanted. Hm. What do you want? Pepperoni? Hawaiian?"

"Soup," Mary says. Sherri laughs.

"Nobody delivers soup!"

Mary tries very hard not to make a face. "Then we'll go shopping."

Sherri gets very serious very quickly. "You're not allowed out- side. Isn't it obvious? The scream last night was a distraction. Hm. Antonio will get you."

Mary scowls. "Not in broad daylight, he won't. I'm getting dressed, and then we'll go."

She pulls a very pretty day dress out of Richmond's closet and tries not to think about to whom it might have once belonged. Maybe Richmond keeps whatever old girl-friends leave behind. Maybe he needs mementos to keep track of everyone he's ever lost. Maybe he's afraid of forgetting them if he doesn't have something to catalogue them with. It's a convenient backstory.

Mary resists the urge to dig into the back of the wardrobe to see if he's hoarding any old corsets, Regency gowns, or panniers. Sherri watches with the air of a puppy determined to guard the henhouse from a generations- old wily fox. She remains unconvinced by the relative safety of Mary's plan, and plies Mary with the offer of takeout, again. It's a bit rude, offering to spend Richmond's money so willy- nilly, and Mary doesn't like it.

It takes perusing through the Yellow Pages, looking up the near- est grocery store, for Mary to realize that the whole of Night City has only one pizzeria, one Chinese food restaurant, and one French one. And nothing else.

She suddenly very desperately longs for a curry. When they make their tottery way to the store a few blocks away—Mary leaning on Sherri—she does her utmost best to assemble one with the bizarre assortments of foods available in the supermarket. But it is impossible. There are pyramids of oranges and cereal boxes, but no Greek- style yogurt. There are shelves of chips and cookies in shiny colorful wrappers, but no rice cakes, no curry mixes, no condensed coconut milk. If it isn't recognizable instantly from once glance of a camera, or if it doesn't fall down artfully, it's not included among the props on the shelves.

Mary settles on buying some Campbell's soup cans, and when they get back, Sherri orders a pizza with

Richmond's money any-way. That's more than just rude, but Mary doesn't want to think ill of Sherri, so she decides not to think about it at all. Mary cooks slowly, exhausted and hurting and longing for quiet.

Quiet is pretty much the exact opposite of what she gets. Sherri plays with Richmond's electric fireplace and turns the TV on and off and on and off. She doesn't help Mary cook or clean up, and wrinkles her nose again, this time not cutely, at the soup. When the pizza arrives, she plops it down onto the table between them and doesn't offer Mary any. She hunches over the box, leaning on her elbows—Mary's grandmother would have smacked her arms with a metal spoon—and eats with her mouth open.

"So, you and Richmond," Sherri says, chomping around her pizza. "Fast."

"Not compared to some girls- of- the- week, I bet," Mary hazards, curious about the others that might have come before her.

"None of them moved in right away." "I had nowhere else to go. Richmond's just being kind."

"Hm."

"You had nowhere else to go, either, may I remind you."

"But I didn't jump into his bed, either."

Mary snaps her teeth closed before the urge to blurt, "*But you would if he'd have you!*" takes control. Instead, she nods in agreement and has a few more mouthfuls of soup.

Sherri makes a few more vaguely hurtful comments about who Mary thinks she is, coming into Richmond's life so quickly. They're the sort of cutting comments a young girl with crush makes to someone older and far more suitable to her target than she, so maybe Mary shouldn't take it so personally. But they sting all the same. Mary always thought that she'd be Sherri's friend.

By the time Mary is done with her soup and feels more like herself again, she is ready for another nap. The sun is setting. And she has decided that Sherri is a little shit.

Just because the brat was fated not to die at the teeth of Antonio doesn't mean she needs to be such a bitch. The kid jealously hordes Richmond's affections, and Mary wouldn't mind at all—the competitive nature of a preteen girl with a silly crush on her immortal, romantic savior—if it wasn't for the fact that Mary knows full well that she's the one who is just a guest star here.

*****

After Sherri goes home, Richmond wakes. He had been holed up in a bolt- space in an old storage cupboard under the staircase. He spends the better part of an hour not meeting her eyes, until Mary grabs him by the front of his shiny red shirt and plants a wet one on him.

"I missed you," Mary says.

"Yeah?"

"It was a looooooong day."

"Yes," Richmond chuckles. "Sherri is very thirteen."

"Yes, she is."

"I wish I could have spent it with you instead." He smiles weakly, but then his eyes drop to her neck and his expression turns hangdog.

"It wasn't your fault, and he's just doing it to make you crawl back to him. It's sick," Mary says. "And you can't get all depressed and blame yourself right away. You are not responsible for the actions of others, especially an asshole like Antonio."

"*All* depressed?" he echoes.

"Moderation, my dear blood- sucker," she admonishes teasingly. Richmond actually grins.

"Moderation. Very well. I'll try, Mary. For you, I will."

"I know," Mary says. "You will because I asked. That's how you're written."

"Written!" Richmond says and laughs. "My amazing Mary, you have the most interesting imagination!"

"Trust me when I say that you don't know even *less* than the half of it."

"What does that mean? Are you going to tell me why you know us all so well?"

Mary considers it for about three whole seconds. Then she shakes her head. "Maybe another time. Later."

"Okay," Richmond allows. "Later." The minute he says it, Mary realizes her mistake. She has given Richmond, the ultimate undead detective, a mystery and a clue. He will be paying closer attention now, weighting every word, judging every action. Well, let him—maybe telling him that he's a TV character is exactly what he needs to jar him out of his emotional rut. Or maybe it will destroy him completely. The existential puzzle is already turning Mary into a mental mess ... what would it be like, she wonders, on the other side. What would it be like to find out that you're not *real*?

Yeah. Mary can't let Richmond know, not that. At least not yet. He's not ready. But maybe by the time he discovers it himself— maybe the very *act* of discovering it himself—

will help him accept it more easily. She decides that she won't encourage him in this investigation, but she won't dissuade him either. If, *when*, he figures it out, that's when she'll deal with crossing that burning bridge, or whatever the metaphor is.

They spend the evening indoors, watching bad b- list vampire movies on his almost pornographically large television, and eating microwave popcorn and tensing at every sound from outside. When Mary finally crashes halfway through a space- vampire flick, Richmond cuddles her close and rests his chin on the back of her neck and listens to her heart beating, slow and steady. Mary smiles and pretends that she is still asleep.

Her heart feels fit to bursting for this awkward, haunted man, and she thinks she'd like it very much if she was the one to finally help him fill out his own skin, become the confident, intelligent person that is just lurking beneath the uncertainty and rigid morality.

She could be the original character she's always tried to write into her own scripts, the scripts that she now knows Mr. Geary was laughing at and tossing into the trash.

Screw you, Mary thinks. *I got it my way after all.* When dawn comes, Mary is woken by the chill of the room. Richmond is wrapped around her, but it's not like he exudes any body heat, not like her vanishingly few furnace- in- disguise ex- boyfriends. She wriggles out of his embrace, this time without the need to nip his nose, and goes into the bedroom and makes sure all the blinds are as shut as they can go, and then sleep- drags him to bed. Sweaty and energized by the exercise, she has a shower and finishes up the last of the cheese pizza and takes three more iron pills and one of those sleep- inducing painkillers.

When she goes back into the bedroom to cuddle back in with Richmond, Antonio is sitting at the foot of the bed, stroking Richmond's calf through the silk sheets.

"That's ... a bit creepy," Mary says, because it's not a gesture she would have attributed to the character. At all. "Also, how did you get in here during the day?"

Antonio smiles, gives a little eyebrow waggle that says, "I have my ways," and then holds out his hand for Mary to take.

She seriously contemplates running instead. Turning on her heel and speeding across the living room and down the stairs to the sun- drenched street outside, booking it all the way to the police station where Police Chief Ironhorse works, a man who knows Richmond and can be trusted to take care of his friends, even if he doesn't approve of Richmond's vigilantism.

But she can't go any faster than a tender limp. She is still tired from the last time Antonio drank her blood, and the pain pill is kicking in, making her eyes heavy. And she is still so battered from being hit by the van. If she ran now, she wouldn't escape. She would only make Antonio mad, or worse, excited.

The balls of her feet itch with the urge to run, the muscles in her back and arms tighten in anticipation of a fight. She sucks in a deep breath and lets it all out and hangs her head, miserable. There really is no way out of this. Mary has always written scripts where the heroine is helpless, where she does not have the physi- cal strength to beat back Antonio, where she isn't witty enough to outfox him.

She thought that would show Antonio to be a stronger villain, a more powerful character. For the first time, Mary really knows what it means to be utterly helpless. And it doesn't make Antonio a strong character. It makes him a *bully*.

"Not in here," she whispers and turns away, goes back out to the living room and sits down in the armchair. Because if she's going to swoon again, she would prefer to be propped up in a chair instead of being dropped to the cold cement floor.

Antonio follows, a dark specter in the corner of her eye. He moves like he's gliding, and Mary wonders if they achieve that with a dolly in production. Mary puts her hands in her lap and tilts her chin up to look Antonio in the eye. He leans down, braces himself on either arm of the chair with fingers bent into claws.

"I'm asking you," she says, softly, "to please not do this."

"Ah, but that's part of the fun," Antonio drawls. "It's hardly punishment if you want it, isn't it?"

Cold fear prickles along Mary's neck, sweat pooling at the bot- tom of her spine. She is having trouble breathing She's sucking on air and filling her lungs, but it seems to be devoid of oxygen. Her head is light and she thinks, *Don't faint, oh God, don't become a fainter now.* She sinks down in the chair a bit, can't help it. She feels nauseous, stomach rolling, hating the soup from earlier. She is chill with terror. "Is there any way I can convince you that this path is only going to push Richmond further away?" Mary asks, knowing the answer already.

Antonio grins. It is not a very nice grin at all. It looks like a knife. He kneels, pushes her thighs apart and nestles in between them. He grabs both her wrists in one hands and pulls her arms out of the way, then pushes up the pretty dress in the other.

Mary loses it. She tries to bring her right leg up to slam her knee against Antonio's head, but he learns fast, won't be rejected in the same way twice. He seizes her knee and digs in his fingernails painfully. She flails, trying to crawl up, back away over the chair or over the arms, brings up her left foot and digs her heel into Antonio's throat, but he is tough and fast, and she is slammed back into the chair, lungs driven hard against her ribs. Light sparkles under her eyelids and her world spins.

She wheezes, lungs burning, yearning desperately for air. Antonio's lips are there, bruising, brutal. His tongue is dry and cold, a revolting piece of dead flesh in her mouth. Mary coughs and gags. His lips seal around hers and she tries to breathe in through her nose, but she can't get enough, not enough, and the edges of her vision gray and blur. She is pushing on his shoulders, but it's not working and she can feel herself slipping, slipping down, down ...

He pulls away and she sucks on the air. Her whole torso is burning with the lack of oxygen, the strangling effort to breathe, and the bruises that both the Craft Services van and Antonio have inflicted. She coughs once, a weak, pathetic sort of sound that she hates, *hates*.

Antonio watches every rise and fall of her chest as if it's the most interesting bit of theatre he's even had the privilege to attend. She stays very still, not wanting to give him any excuse to renew his assault. She is cowed. She is conquered, and she knows it.

It is terrifying. Antonio sinks back down onto his knees. Mary closes her eyes and tries not to squirm. If she can't escape, she can at least be dignified. He sets his teeth against the inside of her thigh and Mary lets out one small, desperate sob.

Chapter Six:
Unauthorized Road Trips
are the Best Kind

Richmond wakes at sunset. Mary wakes soon after to the feel of him shaking her shoulder, the sound of his voice, high and tight with genuine panic.

He fetches water, pain pills, iron pills, and insists that they go to the hospital. Mary shakes her head, grabs his hand and brings it slowly, shakily to her mouth, kissing the knuckles there one by one by one.

"Fuck Antonio," she says. "Let's leave the city."

"Leave it?" Richmond gasps. He jerks his hand away and his eyes go wide, like he's never contemplated it. Never thought about running away. Just leaving the place where the man who torments him also resides.

Idiot. Mary tries very hard to hold on to the affectionate warmth she used to feel when confronted with his endearing obliviousness.

"It's a big world," Mary says. "You could show it to me. I've never been to Paris."

"Paris smells bad."

"hten Venice."

"And run into Antonio's harem?"

"Fair enough. What about you take me to where you grew up, then? I would love to see Kenya in the—"

"No."

"Richmond ... " Mary lays a careful, comforting hand on his arm. "Your weekly mysteries will keep. We can take a night flight to Europe."

"What about Sherri?"

"She's in school. She might actually stay in classes for a whole week, for once."

Richmond looks dubious. "But what will we do?"

"Play tourist. Eat at expensive restaurants. Sneak into museums at night. Have fun."

He scowls.

"Oh, come on," she wheedles. "You're allowed to have fun.

Solving mysteries can't be the only reason you exist."

Only, of course, it is. In the end, Richmond is bound by the show's tag line—Night City, where justice bites back. the whole of his existence, the last few decades of his life, all of it was just a precursor to this, this moment in time, where Richmond DuNoir lives in Night City and metes justice down on the criminal rabble because he feels that he has to make up for the evil of his own existence.

Like there is a cosmic scale out there and the tipping point can't ever come, and Richmond is personally responsible for keeping the grains of evil off the plate he occupies. He isn't as concerned with keeping the good plate populated, as long as there is more there than on the evil side. As many good grains can slip off as they want— innocents can die, and Richmond won't even look up.

Panic seizes Mary. She surges up, burning through what little strength she's recovered. She grabs the front of his pants, the only clothing she can reach from her position slumped in the chair, and her fingers curl into his pockets.

"Please," she begs. "Let's just go for a drive at least."

That seems to work. Richmond has never been able to resist a plea from a damsel in distress. And Mary sure as heck is in distress. Richmond spends the next hour shunting sleeping supplies and spare clothes and bottles of water and what little food and blood bottles he has in the apartment downstairs to his car. He comes back for her, wraps her up in the comforter that was thrown over the back of the leather chair, carries her down the stairs, and dashes for the car. He checks under the chassis, in the trunk, in the back seat.

"No Antonio?" Mary asks, but she asks with a smile, teasing. "No Antonio!" he crows.

He climbs in, puts a bottle of blood in the cup holder, makes sure Mary is buckled in, and then drives like hell. Mary's stomach burbles with joy as he pulls onto a highway on-ramp. And suddenly they are in a dead end alley. Richmond stops.

"You have got to be kidding me," Mary hisses. She clambers out of the car, pulling the blanket around her like a cloak and goes out to touch the wall. It is covered in graffiti. Graffiti, when looked at from far enough away, resolves itself into an image of a highway leading across the shoreline of Night City, a trompe-l'œil. "It's a goddamn matte painting!"

She touches it—yes, it's solid. She bites her lip and tries not cry. Richmond is still seated behind the wheel, looking confused. He rolls down the window.

"Mary?"

"Is there no other way out of this goddamned backlot?"

"Backlot?"

"Set! Studio! Location! There has to be a way to get out of Night City!"

"Is that what you were trying to do?" He blinks. There seems to be some sort of internal struggle going on behind his eyes, a war between what he wants and what he's made to want. Mary silently cheers for the human, the person side to win. "Why would we ever want to leave Night City?" he asks, but his teeth are clenched and his knuckles are going pale around the steering well. He is puffing like he is running a marathon or wrestling a titan.

Mary marches up to the car and slams her hands down on the hood. "You were born in Kenya for chrissake! You used to live in Italy! You got your European name in France! How did you get here from there? What about Berlin? Salzburg? Prague? Moscow? All the places that Antonio took you? How do we get there, Richmond?"

Richmond whines and holds his head. It looks like he is trying to keep it from splitting open. "There's only one highway that leads out of town. But why? Why would we ... want to leave ... I don't..."

"Because we're going to run, Richmond. We're going to run the hell away from City by Night. We're going to leave. You are going to dictate the terms of your own existence for once."

Richmond shudders once, all over, and goes very, very still. He slumps like a puppet with its strings cut. Mary curls her hands into fists and watches, because she wants to see it when it happens, she wants to remember the moment where Richmond becomes a man and not a bunch of words on paper.

She wants to remember the moment where she wins.

And then Richmond sits up. His face is clear of the dollish confusion that he's been wearing since he met Mary. He looks, for the first time, like a man with independent agency. His shoulders are back, relaxed in a way that she hasn't seen in an age, his smile confident, his eyes dark and content.

"Run. Yeah," he says. He reaches across the seat and opens the passenger door. "Get in. I know a place."

Mary kisses him as she buckles her seatbelt, and he tastes like victory.

*****

They drive all through the first night, Mary dozing in fits, accepting water when Richmond tips the bottle up one handed for her, nibbling at the french fries he grabs at a faceless fast food place beside where he fills up the tank.

But better than all of that, they talk. Really talk. Not in exposition or in the stilted dialogue meant to further the plot. They chat, topics wandering aimlessly, sentences

85

trailing off, half-finished, thoughts left to dangle. Richmond spends a whole hour talking about how to create the perfect hunting spear, and then wallows in homesickness for the first time Mary has ever seen. He is so depressed, Mary fears that he'll throw himself into the sun in the morning. Part of her takes joy in the depth of his emotion. the other part feels like a stinking asshole for forcing the unpleasantness that she's brought down on him.

In the end, she leaves him to his silent contemplation, because pain is a good builder of character, of moral strength. They drive in quiet until dawn, and then Richmond pulls over into a convenient copse of thick pine trees beside the road, kills the engine and gives Mary a good-day kiss. He burrows down in the footwell of the back seat under a heavy rubber blanket that completely blocks out the light. It's a good thing he doesn't toss and turn in his sleep. Mary makes sure all the doors are locked and can't resist the pull of the painkillers down into oblivion.

Richmond is driving again when she wakes, and the sun is just set, the sky still tangerine and gold at the far horizon. His cheeks are a wee bit sunburnt, his lips cracked and chapped, but he is wearing thick leather gloves, a brimmed black cap, and big dark glasses. Mary's stomach grumbles, which they both take for a good sign, and they pull over at another faceless fast food place—not a brand logo in sight—for a chance to use the washrooms to freshen up, wash their faces, and get Mary something with lots of red meat in it. They drive like this for two more days until Richmond finally pulls them off the interstate and onto a rundown back road.

"This was Sherri's parents' cottage," Richmond explains slowly. "Hers, really, but she can't inherit yet. I'm the executor of her estate. Antonio can't possibly know about it."

Mary winces. the last sentence has pretty much assured that Antonio does. And of course, the place Richmond has taken them is associated with the show; she was hoping that he would have headed for a real place, like Chicago or Washington, somewhere big enough to be lost in a crowd. Maybe even to the real Toronto, if it exists here. the thought that it might not, that perhaps Toronto has been consumed by Night City, freaks her out a little bit so she puts that thought away. One of these nights, she's going to ask Richmond to point out Night City on a map. But not tonight.

Because the process of breaking away from City by Night is slow, and probably painful for Richmond. this cottage is on the outer orbit of the program, held by only the loosest gravity of mention on air. So Mary will keep her peace and be content to stay, for now. Tomorrow they will try to break free.

the cottage they pull up to is more on the ground than it is upright. the screen on the front door has swung off its hinges and is rusting contentedly on the dipping and pockmarked porch, but the inner door is still solidly locked and bolted shut. the shutters are listing sideways, leaving cracks large enough to let in dangerous shafts of piercing sunlight. There are crumbling, age-whitened animal droppings all over the equally age-whitened Muskoka chairs.

The driveway, if there ever was one, has been overtaken with knee-high weeds, and the remains of an outhouse lay in pieces on the ground around the dark pit. A canoe, mounted upside down under an over- hang and a hopeful tarpaulin, has been speared by a fallen beam.

Mary is dubious about this building's ability to keep anyone out, let alone an angry Elder Vampire, but Richmond is satisfied.

Not for the first time, Mary realizes that the man she is in love with is sort of, well... dumb. But his common sense is building, brick by brick, thought by thought. Soon enough, she'll have him thinking logically.

They park, and Richmond disembarks and goes up to the front door, takes a rusty key from his pocket and jiggles it in the equally rusty lock. Mary hunches down in her seat and tries not to jump at shadows. She half expects dark straight hair and black, vindictive eyes fringed with false lashes to appear in her line of sight any second now. They don't, and after Richmond shoos a bear out of the cottage and back into the woods, he unloads Mary and all their gear into the building. It smells of wet fur, old wood, and dust. At least the walls are completely intact, even if Richmond has to use his heavy rubber blanket to cover a hole in the roof. Out the back window, Mary can see a stony path leading out into the darkness; she can't see the gray, pebbly beach that this part of the country is prone to, but she can hear the distinctive calm lap of the lake against the rocks.

Richmond confesses that he is desperately hungry and apologizes for not having something better for Mary. He points Mary to the cereal bars they'd bought at the last gas station before speeding off into the forest to catch his own dinner. He promises her a cup of hot tea when he gets back, that he'll get the old iron fireplace up and running, and rabbit stew to boot. There's a few hours yet before sunrise, and Mary trusts that he knows his way around enough to get back.

He is gone in the next heartbeat and Mary thrills to how ... well, cool, that is. She eats a cereal bar and putters a bit, improvising a broom out of a fallen branch and laying their sleeping gear in the cleaned space.

The crunch of feet on dry grass grabs Mary's attention and she totters out onto the porch to ask what Richmond caught.

Of course, it's not Richmond. Of course not. Antonio is standing on the bottom step, grinning.

"You know, you can still be evil without being an utter prick," Mary says.

Antonio's backhand is so fast Mary's lip is bleeding before she even feels the pain of the strike. She staggers to the side, barely catches herself on the porch railing. She spits the blood in her mouth onto the grass. There. that, at least, is a bit of her that Antonio will never get.

She does not look up. "What are you doing here?"

From the corner of her eye, she can see Antonio lick his lips. His eyes, framed by those fake lashes, are all blown pupil, vibrant yellow, and bloodshot whites. They're focused on the trickle burning down her chin.

"I've come to collect what is rightfully mine."

"No."

"Richmon' is my property, and as his, you are also mine."

"No."

"Come here, Contrary Mary." He holds out his hand. Mary swallows hard and hates, hates that there is nothing she can do, literally nothing, but take it.

Chapter Seven :
If You Can't Beat 'em, Get a Bigger Stick

Mary wakes to the sound of groaning hinges. She can tell by the weight of the fabric that she is wrapped in a blanket on

the floor of the cabin. When she opens her eyes, she can see the silhouette of Richmond crouched down by the iron stove, arm stuck inside to lay tinder. There is a spark of light and Richmond sits back, carefully watching the fire grow.

"Now what?" he asks.

Mary doesn't bother wasting breath to ask how he knows she was awake. She just licks her lips and says, "We go somewhere further. Somewhere you've never been before."

"But why?" Richmond asks.

"Yes, that, exactly," Mary says. "Why. Good question. It's one you should ask more. Why? Why stay? Why listen to him? Why give in?"

"Why not give in?" His voice is so miserable, Mary actually struggles to sit up.

Her head is swimming, but she shuffles over and wraps her arms around his shoulders and presses her cheek against his neck and stares into the belly of the stove, reveling in the dry warmth is spreads across her face. "Because."

"Because?"

"Because you are a good person and you deserve better than the hand you were dealt."

"But what if I'm not? What if I'm not a good person?"

"You are," Mary whispers. "I know you are."

"My amazing Mary," he murmurs and turns his face to her, kissing her softly, gently. He is searching for something in the kiss, an answer, a truth, Mary isn't sure, but she opens up, gives him everything, anything he wants. He has fed enough to be able to make love and they do, on the worn blanket and dusty floor in front of a feeble fireplace. Mary whimpers at each touch that lands on a bruise, arching against his cold skin in the futile, desperate search for heat. "You make me strong," he says as they lie together, tangled in the afterglow. "You make me think. You're like a drug, but the opposite of a drug. My mind gets clearer when you're around. I can see better. Things make more sense. And it terrifies me."

"Why?"

"Because I think I'm becoming reliant on you. I feel stupid when you're not here and I don't like it. I don't want to be stupid. But... what if something happens to you?"

"Nothing will happen to me."

"What if you leave me?"

"I'm not going anywhere," Mary says and rolls over to pull him close, to cradle his head against her chest and run a hand over his hair and the nape of his neck, soothing.

"What if he takes you from me?"

"We won't let him."

Richmond sits up suddenly, arms braced on either side of her, looking down with an intent, lustful, possessive expression on his face. "I could make sure of it," he whispers. "I've never done it before, but I know how."

It takes Mary a second to figure out what he means. "Oh," she whispers.

And this is something special, because never, not once, has Richmond ever offered it to anyone else. the cardinal rule of writing Richmond DuNoir is that he would never, ever love someone enough to afflict vampirism on them. Or hate them enough, either. that is the one thing that Richmond would never do.

And here he is, offering it, breaking his own mold. Thinking for himself.

"I'd never have to be without you again," he insists, gathering Mary up and holding him against his own chest, nuzzling against the scabs that have barely closed after Antonio's attentions. "I could have you forever."

Mary closes her eyes and leans her head back, a silent invitation. *Yes, yes, yes*, she thinks. But then she thinks about home. About how vampires aren't real where she comes from. About how, if she does this, she might never get to go back.

She hasn't cared too much about getting back home, but suddenly finding that the choice might be taken away from her forever, she panics.

"No," she says and pushes him away.

"No?" Richmond leans back, and his eyes are glowing, the pupils wide, his face slack with lust and incomprehension. "What do you mean, no?"

"I ... " Mary stammers. "I can't. Not if ... not if I'm just your crutch."

"But I love you!"

It is the first time he has said it out loud and it should fill her with warm fuzzies to hear it. But he's made it sound like a justification instead of a confession. that is not romantic.

"I love you, too," she says, and she's pretty sure she means it. "But this, you're only doing this because you are afraid. Antonio has made it pretty clear that he can take me away from you the moment he chooses, and that scares the ever loving crap out of you, doesn't it?" He casts his eyes downward, ashamed. "So what are you going to do? Exactly what he wants you to do. You're going to break your vow and make another vampire. And then Antonio wins."

Richmond stands and begins to pace back and forth across the small cabin, wringing his hands.

"I don't know what to do, Mary!" he wails dramatically. "this is hard. I've never had to make a choice like this before and I don't know how to do it. I don't like it."

"Making choices is never easy," Mary agrees. "Especially the kind that matter. They're not supposed to be easy."

"I want you," he says. "I want to stay with you forever."

"You can."

"For your forever, sure. But not mine."

"Richmond ..."

"I could do it, you know," he says, and throws himself down onto the blanket beside her. Before she knows what's happening, he's got her rolled onto her back, one hand behind her head to protect it from the hard floor, the other sliding up her inner thigh, sending sparks of frisson up Mary's spine to fog her brain. "I could just do it if I wanted to."

"You could," Mary agrees, sighing into his hair as he leans down and kisses her neck, sucking a hickey onto her skin. "But you won't."

"Oh, no?" he snarls. His teeth prick against her flesh. "No."

"Why not?"

"Because I've asked you not to."

Richmond stiffens, his fingers ceasing their exploration, his lips jerking away from her neck.

"Damn you," he hisses resentfully. He rolls away and puts his back to her.

"Are you pouting?" Mary asks, rolling over herself to spoon him from behind.

"No," he says sullenly.

Mary kisses the back of his neck in an effort to stifle a chuckle.

She doesn't quite succeed.

"Don't laugh!" Richmond says. "It's not fair."

"Life isn't fair," Mary says, rattling off the idiom before she really realizes she's saying it. It's a rote attempt at comfort, but it abruptly strikes her that it's just as applicable to her life as his. Life isn't fair. Her boss hated her, and her coworkers barely knew she existed. She just wanted to belong and nobody would open the door for her.

And now she's here and it's everything she's ever wanted, and it's still frustrating and painful and harsh. It's not perfect. It's not fair. But life rarely is.

That's literally just life. And it's up to you to make it good, and surround yourself with kind people over the charming, toxic ones, and to open your own damn doors.

"How about later?" Richmond asks suddenly. He reaches up and takes her hand and threads his fingers between hers. "Can I do it later?"

"Maybe," Mary says. Maybe when I've given up all hope of ever going home. Maybe when I've resigned myself to staying here. Maybe when you are ready enough to live with me as an equal, not as a depend- ant. Maybe when you don't need me so much.

"Amazing Mary," Richmond says. He turns to face her, wiggling on the blanket and runs one hand down her back, across her rump, and finishes what he had started.

Mary laughs into his kiss and arches against his palm and makes sure he knows how much she approves of his work ethic.

*****

They sleep all day in the rotting cottage and drive all night. They hit Canada at around three a.m. and breeze through the border crossing. Mary gives into a ridiculous urge to tell him about her teenaged-self's fantasy of staying in a honeymoon suite overlooking the Falls. Richmond thinks it's a wonderful, splendid idea, and they buy cheap plastic rings at a tourist shop on Lundy's Lane and flash them under the nose of the concierge to make sure they can get the suite. It has a Jacuzzi and a heart-shaped bed.

Mary orders nearly a hundred bucks worth of room service, which considering this is a honeymoon suite in Niagara Falls, isn't a lot of food. She has a huge steak and a big salad, her appetite back with a vengeance, while Richmond takes a shower. She opens all the windows to let the food smell out, and they both sip something red out of wine glasses as the Jacuzzi fills. It is lovely and romantic and exactly what Richmond needs to get out of his funk, and what Mary needs to really get to know Richmond as something more than just that man she watched on TV on Thursday nights.

They sleep in exhausted bliss all day, curtains pulled tight against the glory of the falls. At sunset, they both leap awake, startled by the sound of gunfire. Richmond is on his feet, snarling, facing the door before Mary can even process the flat cracking sound. And then he straightens and turns to stare at the wall of curtains with a puzzled look furrowing his eyebrows. He goes over to the floor-to-ceiling windows and draws the curtains back—a dazzling flash of green, followed by a flower-shaped burst of blue erupt against the darkening sky.

Mary laughs. "Fireworks!" she says.

Richmond laughs, too; a big, deep belly laugh that shakes his whole body. "I've been living in Night City too long!" he says, and laughs some more.

He stumbles toward the bed, breath stuttering and eyes squeezed shut. He flops down onto the end of the bed giggling, and Mary laughs along with him until she realizes his giggles are becoming a bit hysterical. As suddenly as he was laughing, his whole body is wracked with sobs. Blood is dripping from his eyes, staining the white duvet, blossoming like rose petals on the expensive cotton.

"Oh, Rich, shhhh," Mary says, pulls his head onto her lap and pets his head like a child.

Richmond cries for a while, and then he crawls up her body, kissing every inch of skin he can reach as he goes, whispering, "I hate him. I can't lose you. I hate him so much. I hate what he did to me. I miss the city. I miss Sherri. I don't want to lose you."

"I'm here, I'm here, I'm not going anywhere," Mary says, and proceeds to show him how very present she is.

They shower together and take a walk through the butterfly conservatory after hours, Richmond fiddling with the security cam- eras enough so they show a loop of empty gardens for the rest of the night. They think about going through one of the late-night horror houses, but decide against it when they hear the chilling recorded screams. Instead, they do the wax museum, and Richmond scoffs at the dummy of Marie Antoinette and tells Mary a ribald story about meeting the doomed queen in the gardens of Versailles one night.

Richmond finishes the last of his bottled blood when they get back, and Mary takes careful stock of all of her wounds in the bathroom mirror—the scrapes are all healed, her face free of bruising finally, and the cuts on her left arm and leg are less red, less swollen, the skin starting to close into a fine white line that looks so visually appealing it could only have been designed by a makeup team. that is one advantage to this place—no scars are ever ugly, unless they're painted on a villain.

They close the curtains again and crawl into bed. Mary is woken by a hand over her mouth sometime after eleven in the morning— she can't see all of the numbers on the digital display over Antonio's thumb.

He pulls her upright by her hair, hand clamped to keep the noise down, and bites her neck right there, clenching harder with his teeth than necessary to punish her. Then, perversely, he holds her still and helps her drink down the glass of water she had left beside the clock. His hand is insistent, and he won't withdraw until the whole glass is gone.

When she's done, he simply lets go. She flops back down onto the mattress, and he vanishes, back out the door she swears Richmond locked, leaving her to gulp through the nausea until exhaustion claims her around one in the afternoon.

Chapter Eight:
How Can You Know When You Won't Even Try?

Mary knows that it's killing Richmond to keep finding her like this, blood dried on wounds, splayed out, and exposed. Antonio never does more than take a few mouthfuls, but the message is clear: there is nowhere Richmond can stow Mary that Antonio can't get into. Richmond doesn't sleep for days, and they drive far out into the countryside, into cities and out again, in circles and squares, up one state and down another, into Canada and back out again.

And still Antonio is there. He is there in the five star hotel. He is there in the police holding cell. He is there at the airport and in the field tent and in the cheap roadside inn.

But Mary gets to travel with Richmond—courteous, interesting, thoughtful Richmond. Mary slowly regains her strength, recovers as much as she is able with someone drinking gulps of her

blood every few nights. Her asphalt burns scab up and flake away. And Richmond talks. He talks about Antonio and what happened, how he's been hunted by the other vampire all his unlife, how he wants to be free of his sadistic shadow, to maybe even be human again.

And slowly, surely, Mary builds up his confidence, his courage, his ego. She tells him he is strong and independent. She tells him he is an adult, and he is free and no one's slave, and slowly Richmond stops walking with his shoulders rounded in, stops peering over his arm when he's said something that offends. Richmond opens up, becomes the sure and steady man that he used to be all those centuries ago; the confident, charming man, wise and free, that Mary has only teasingly glimpsed in flashback segments.

Richmond stops being a character and starts being a person.

She drinks wine with him and he sips on her veins in order to taste the alcohol. ftey have an outdoor picnic at night, and it is romantic, and she only thinks once that while this is nice, there is no way any relationship can last if all they're doing is romantic things on the run. It needs familiarity, routine, curled up in sock feet in front of the boob tube. But Richmond it able to talk freely and openly about his past, which he rarely gets to do with anyone. Mary gets to hear all about his background, and gloats only a little to herself because the fans on the boards don't get this.

Only her.

This is hers, this part of Richmond. No one elses'.

But she is getting annoyed at being the pawn in his and Antonio's pathetic power struggle. She is exhausted. She should leave Richmond for good, but then Antonio would win, because the only person Richmond has would be him again. And Richmond, in his despair, always turns to his maker for physical comfort. And Mary would probably be killed off the very night she does break it off with Richmond, no longer needed to prove a point.

And who else does Mary have in this world, but Richmond? No one. Nothing.

And no way to get home.

Not that she'd even really tried. With no idea how it happened in the first place, where is she even to begin? Who could expect her to figure this out on her own?

In the five star hotel, after waking up with a hideous hickey and a livid oozing slash on the inside of her elbow, Mary had plucked up the courage to dial her mother's phone number. Her mother's voice answered the phone, but insisted that she had no daughter named Mary and that she's going to call the police.

Mary had hung up.

In the cheap motel, Mary had called her production studio, and an automated voice said that the number was not in service. Mary uses the inordinately expensive Internet service in the suite to Google City by Night and Richmond DuNoir and Crispin Okafor, and gets nothing but a few outdated police APBs and a restaurant guide.

She gave up making phone calls after that.

Because of Antonio, Richmond hasn't taken any real amount of blood from her in nearly a week now, which also means no sex— fingers and mouths are great, but the deep connection of actual penetration is something both of them miss. Mary wonders if the shiny is going to rub off the relationship if they don't get some nooky soon. Making out is wonderful, but it's not quite doing it anymore.

They try a cabin by an out of season ski resort next. The cabins have no power running to them in the summer, so Richmond leaves her on the porch as he goes back to the car to find a flash- light. Nighttime in the country is light enough for him to make his way through the building, but not Mary. She hesitates by the door, decides the interior is too dark for her, and turns back around to wait on the rattan sofa by the door. Antonio, of course, is standing at the bottom of the stairs.

Mary sighs. "Seriously, how are you doing this? Where do you sleep? Where do you wash your hair? Do you drive?"

"Come here, Contrary Mary ..." he says, hand outstretched.

"And if I say no?"

Antonio backhands her before she ever sees him move. Mary crashes into the wall, her lip split, and then Antonio is right up in her face.

"You know," Mary says, probing at her lip with her tongue. It stings. "You're still being an utter prick. I don't know if you were going to try to address that, but this isn't working in your favor."

Antonio dips his head and licks the blood off her chin. From off screen, Richmond shouts, "Antonio!"

Antonio jerks back and glares at Richmond standing at the edge of the forest wielding a broken tree branch like a spear.

"Finally," Mary says.

"Richmon', my pet. Come, come, let's share her." Antonio licks up the side of her face, wet and cold, and Mary shudders.

"Do not touch her!"

Antonio scowls. "You do not tell me what to do, my son."

"I do now. I'm no son of yours. And she is not the pawn in your power games. I want nothing to do with you anymore, so just leave us be!"

Weakly, head still spinning, Mary pumps her fist in the air and says, "Whoo-hoo. that's my man. Gurk!" Antonio tightens his hand around her throat.

"Quiet, you troublesome thing," he mutters. "Very well, then," Antonio intones more loudly, meant for Richmond's ears also. "I can see that we are at an impasse in regards to Miss Mary's death. Shall we now dice with her life, my boy?"

Richmond's hands tighten on the spear. Otherwise, he makes no indication that he knows what Antonio is suggesting.

"You have not done it, yet," Antonio says, his voice like warm butter: seductive and playful and rich. "Do you not recall how I did it to you? Or do you fear you will make a mistake?"

"She doesn't want it," Richmond says, but his expression is wavering.

"Ah, but what do you want, Richmon'?"

The temptation is strong for Richmond. Mary can see it in his face. All he would have to do is nod and that would be it. Antonio would strike. Mary would be Antonio's daughter and Richmond would owe his sire even more. They would both be trapped forever, then. Both under the Italian Monster's thumb.

If Mary was going to join the ranks of the undead against her will, she would at least prefer Richmond to be her maker.

"Well?" Antonio prompts into the silence. "What is your answer? This is my final visit, Richmon'. I tire of chasing you all over this wretched continent. Make her as we are, or kill her. Or I will take the choice from you. What do you say?"

"This!" Richmond snarls. He rushes Antonio with the branch. the grip of Antonio's hand vanishes and Mary slumps, sucking on the cool night air. the point of the branch digs into the wall beside Mary's head, making her near jump out of her skin.

"Wah!" she cries. the branch is embedded in the wall, shivering slightly from the impact. ften, shakily, she adds: "Nice aim."

Antonio, of course, is gone. She would have much preferred to see him impaled on the branch, like a butterfly to a corkboard. Richmond lets go of the branch and sinks to his knees. He holds Mary in a fierce hug. "We can't outrun him. And we can't out think him."

"Are you seriously going to fall for that? He speaks five lines of dialogue at you, and you're back to Mister McBroody?"

"Mary, he's right. He's tempting me with the one thing I really want."

"So be the stronger man, say no."

"I tried!"

"Barely."

Richmond runs his hands through her hair, moaning in a dramatically tortured fashion against the skin of her shoulder. "If I cannot keep you in the way that I want, then I don't think I can be with you anymore, Mary."

Mary jerks out of his embrace, staring up at him with wide eyes. "Where is this coming from, all of a sudden?"

"Mary, I should let you go."

"What? No!" Mary insists. "I'm not... I'm not just someone you can discard when it gets too hard. I'm not some girl-of-the- week. I'm not replaceable."

"But if I can't have you the way I want you, then why torture myself by being with you at all?" Richmond insists right back.

"Because he'll kill me. the second you do that, he'll kill me, you know that. Why are you being stupid again?"

"I don't. I'm not."

Mary tries to shove him off, but he clings like a squid. "You are! I won't have any meaning to him anymore, and it would just hurt you. that's all he wants, is to hurt you."

"You can't know that."

Mary reaches up and grabs the sides of his head and forces him to meet her eyes. "I do. I know for certain."

Richmond lets go of her finally and surges up to his feet, exploding with rage. "How? Why? You say that you know so much, but you never say why!"

Mary refuses to be cowed by his theatrics. "Because you'd never believe me."

"You say that, and it means nothing!"

"Richmond ..."

"No! I just..." He paces away across the porch, hands scrubbing at his skull, like he can get in at the ideas Mary's planted, the thoughts and the personality, and yank them out like a cancer. "I've wrapped my whole life around you, and I can't even figure out why! I haven't solved a mystery in a week! My gods, I even abandoned Sherri for you! Who are you?"

He's making me sound like some goddamned self-inserted fan character. I am not some... some parasite! "I'm the person who's trying to give you some goddamned character agency!" she yells.

"And what the hell is that even supposed to mean!" he roars back, voice echoing into the night.

"Fine! Then I'm the person who lo—"

"Don't you dare say that to me!" Richmond's eyes flare yellow, glowing with his fury. "You selfish ... woman!"

Mary is so startled by his intense anger at how, for the first time, it is directed in its entirety at her, that she is literally shocked into tears. "I ... I'm Mary," she blubbers, trying to swallow back the utter despair she feels, the defeat. She had tried so hard. She had tried for Richmond. It wasn't selfish, it wasn't. It was for Richmond, all of it, everything. It was all for him, to make him better, to fix the flaws written into him, to make him balanced and calm and whole.

"Just, Mary."

Richmond runs his hands through his hair, frustrated. He turns his back to her.

There is a long, long moment, and Mary knows that she has lost, finally, when his shoulders slump and he takes the car keys out of his pocket. "We're going back to Night City."

"Richmond ..."

"Don't try to talk me out of it. I'll wrap you up in the blanket and lock you in the trunk if I have to. this isn't working. We can't outrun him. I'm going back. I belong there."

"You don't understand what you're saying. You don't need it."

"Then you don't know me at all," Richmond spits. "I love that city. I was made for that city."

Mary covers her mouth with her hand, too shocked to speak. And then the words surge up out of her like a torrent, a last desperate attempt. "Don't say that. You weren't. You're a person, Richmond, not a ... a plot device! God, say anything but that. You don't know what it means ..."

He whirls around to face her, fists tight around the jangling key chain. "Because you won't tell me! There's a mystery there, I can see it, but I can't figure it out! I can't stand it, Mary, I just can't! You can't keep this secret from me!"

"Richmond ... it would shatter you. It's for your own good." She holds her hand out for him. He doesn't take it.

"Selfish," he says again, and it feels like a slap across the face, more painful than anything Antonio has ever meted out. "We need to get you to a hospital."

Only then does he take her hand. He hauls her to her feet, and when Mary tries to hold on, to keep her fingers twined around his, he shakes his own free and walks back to the car, a few paces ahead and not looking back, a confident Orpheus. Mary can only stumble along the rocky path beside him, night blind, miserable, and defeated.

*****

They only have to drive for one night. He takes Mary directly to the hospital in Night City. They have gone nearly a complete circle and they are both tired. the nurses cut out her stitches and give her more pain pills and tsk over her health, her papery skin, and dark eye bruises, and tell Richmond to go a little easier on her. They both start, wondering if the doctor knows what Richmond is, but no, the doctor referring to all the kinky sex that he assumes is leaving the marks all over her. They hook her up to a few drips to get her nutrient levels back up, and Richmond sits beside her bed, remaining stalwartly silent. He won't even hold her hand.

But Mary isn't going to give up. "You just have to stand up to him," Mary says softly. "Just tell him to screw off and he will. As soon as he realizes that you're not going to play the game any- more ..." She makes a frustrated sound. "You just have to stop playing the game! It's so easy!"

"Mary," Richmond says softly, and Mary swings her head around, because she knows this tone of voice. She's heard this tone before. And she doesn't like it.

"No," she says. "Stop trying." "No."

"I can't hear it any more ... I'm tired."

"So what? Either I shut up about Antonio, or you'll ... you'll what, leave? Never come see me? Never talk to me? Ever again?"

"Yes."

"He'll kill me the second you do." "You don't know that."

"I do. I know for absolute certain."

Richmond storms out of the hospital room. She shouldn't be surprised, he's still an utter drama queen after all. Nobody's perfect, but it is shocking and almost hurtful all the same. And when Mary is discharged an hour later, alone, she doesn't bother looking for him. She just gets dressed and walks out of the emergency exit and wonders if she can hail the same cabbie as before.

This time, she'll go somewhere else, somewhere far away; she'll just tell him to drive. If Richmond wants to come find her, he can do it after his hissy fit. One bloody hour back in Night City and Richmond is back to acting like that spoiled, insecure scaredy-cat he was written as. And to think she used to find him charmingly vulnerable!

She is sick to death of television characters and their denseness. She doesn't even hear the car skid round the corner, but she sees Antonio grinning from the driver's seat, hears Richmond's agonized

"Mary!" from across the parking lot.

She doesn't feel herself go over the hood, up the windshield, roll on the roof, and back down, but she assumes that's what happened because she's suddenly on the road and watching the car's tail lights fade away into a sudden burst of pouring rain. And everything hurts. It hurts to open her eyes. It hurts to close them. It hurts to breathe.

Pathetic fallacy, she thinks. *It's pathetic.*

"No!" Richmond moans, and she feels his hands on her shoulders, his mouth already on her neck. "I won't let you die."

"Oh, for God's sake," Mary manages to say around the agony in her chest. "Stop being so fucking melodramatic." She should be scared, but all she really feels is exasperation.

"But, Mary!"

"No," she says. "Don't do it to me. I don't want it."

"Mary—"

"Will you do it to me when you told Antonio no?"

"But I need to be near you! I want you to stay! I can make you stay!"

"I will be very cross if I wake up dead."

"Mary ..."

"Good. Bye, Richmond."

"But I never found out how you knew about me! Who you are!"

"Mystery for another week," Mary says, and starts coughing. "Ow," she says. "this drawn out death thing is ridiculous. Richmond?"

"Yes, Mary?" He sounds like he's sobbing. Mary's not sure because she thinks she's got blood in her eyes.

"Could you do the honors? Make it quick?"

"Mary, no," he gasps, really getting into the swing of his angsty parting of the ways. Viewers all over the country must be weeping. A dark-haired shadow appears over his shoulder and Mary urges Richmond to hurry, before Antonio can get in the way.

"Shut up and do it," Mary says. She doesn't add, before I expire of melodrama overload.

She feels his lips on her neck, the soft prick of his fangs brushing against the smooth skin there. It raises goose bumps. "I love you, Mary," he says, smearing the words against her flesh.

Mary isn't quite sure how she feels about that, so says nothing. She closes her eyes and lets go.

Chapter Nine:
The One Where Mary Sues

"Mary?" Richmond asks. He's holding her in his arms. He looks worried.

"Richmond!" she says and surges up for a kiss. Her heart surges in her chest, her breath catches in her throat, which is enough to tell her that she is alive after all! And he hasn't left her!

Yes, there's the familiar hospital ceiling, there's the poke of an IV in the back of her hand, the revolting scent of flowers and people dying all over the rest of the ward. It stinks in here and it's painful and she's alive!

Richmond does not kiss her back. In fact, he looks distinctly uncomfortable, getting his face as far away from her as he can with- out actually dropping her back down into the bed she's lying in.

"That truck hit you pretty hard," Richmond says.

Someone out in the hall shouts, and suddenly, there's a photographer in the room. Richmond is jabbing her in the side with his elbow and telling her to smile. Someone brings in balloons and a mountain of flowers from somewhere to dress up the background, and it isn't until all the media fanfare follows Richmond out of the room—after a kiss right above her temple which makes Mary recoil in confusion—that the nurses can even get inside to explain to Mary that she's been in a coma for eight months.

"Why was he here?" Mary asks. "What city am I in?"

"I dunno, but he seems a sweet young man. Is he a movie star?" the nurse answers. "And Toronto, dear."

It is only the next day when Mary gets the entertainment section of the newspaper given to her by one of the doctors that she under- stands. the headline reads "Amazing Recovery for Dearly Missed 'City' Crew Member! Star On Hand To Welcome Her Home!" In the picture, Mary looks startled. the scar from the stitches is still red and prominent, just below Crispin's dark lips.

Mary feels sick. She can't even bear to look at the picture of Crispin Okafor kissing her forehead tenderly, an act, let alone read the rest of the article.

*****

The first night after Mary wakes up, she has an orderly sneak in some Thai food for her. Every night until she's released, she bribes the boy with autographs from

Crispin—who visits with a camera crew nearly daily—and collectibles from the show, with anecdotes and sometimes cash, and he brings back some new kind of cuisine from a new restaurant, a new country: sushi, sashimi, stir fry, pad thai, roasted yams, hamburgers, street fries, gazpacho, tacos, curries of every kind and flavor, lamb and shellfish, octopus, and duck.

Her parents come and they hug a lot, and then they go back to the small town they're from and promise to return to help Mary settle back into her apartment. the landlord had been holding it for her, rent-free, because he was a City by Night fan.

During the day, Mary does television and radio interviews for the press, or writes down everything she can remember about her time in that other place, the evolution of Richmond as a character, the revelations and frustrations of living in a fictional place. She hides this under her pillow. It's not for other people. Not yet, anyway.

She does not catch up on the fan fiction, the Wikipedia entries, or IMDB tidbits, or watch the new season. She's quite content to not see or read about Richmond DuNoir and his silly little world for a very long time. Her hospital room becomes a spoiler-free zone. She's let out of the hospital with a ridiculously large settlement package from the studio for the accident, and an offer to have her old job back if she wants it. She doesn't. After that, nobody calls her for interviews any more. She and the studio have milked all the publicity out of the event that they can. She makes an appointment to see Mr. Geary, the showrunner, on the first Monday of the very next month.

She walks with confidence into his office, and his eyes

skitter over her face, circle around the scar on her forehead, and down to the top of his desk.

"Hi, Mary," he says.

"Hi, Mark," she says back. She's feeling vindictive. She likes that he's feeling guilty and squirmy. He should, after the way he treated her, after what happened because of it. He is a manipulative asshole, and she's since learned how to deal with manipulative assholes.

Her boots, the ones she had dropped in front of his office door the day she was hit by the van, are sitting, neatly lined up on the shelf behind his head like some sort of sick inspiration, or a guilty reminder, or a trophy.

She points to them. "Can I have those back?"

"What?" He follows where her fingers are pointing and flushes. "Yes, of course."

He takes them down and hands them to her. She clutches them in her left hand. In her right, she has another brown paper production envelope. this time, there is no script inside, no plot arc suggestions. Only Post-It notes and napkins and spiral ring notebooks filled with everything that happened to her while she has been "away".

Mr. Geary takes the package and goes back to his desk and opens it, silently. He skims over it, flipping pages back and forth, confused, chewing on his bottom lip or raising an eyebrow.

Mary sits down in the chair opposite his desk and waits.

After a long time and three attempts to drink coffee from a cup by his elbow that was empty when Mary walked in, he looks up and puffs out a breath.

"Mary ..." Mr. Geary says slowly, looking up from the wad of messy notes and half-finished sentences to Mary and back again. "Have you watched any of Season Three yet?"

"No. Duh. I was in a coma."

Mr. Geary stands, walks around the desk and motions for her to stand up. Mary does. He takes her gently by the shoulders, turns her all the way around to face the new Season Three poster tacked to the back of the door. There's Richmond, yes, still in the foreground frowning his little eyebrow frown, and the spunky Sherri, a little older and clutching a textbook, beside him, but Antonio has faded into the background, and there is a new woman beside Richmond that Mary has never seen before. She is grinning like a shit, like she's about to cause trouble, and she knows it. She is a bit taller than Mary, a bit thinner, but otherwise her hair looks nearly identical. Her eyes are almost the same shade of blue, but vaguely purple, her freckles painted on to match Mary's.

"Who... who is that?" Mary asks.

"That's Mary," Mr. Geary says, "Mary Trinity. We, uh, we named her after you, you know, for ... in honor... for ..."

"For a publicity stunt?" Mary doesn't even feel sorry when Mr. Geary winces. "Just like Crispin visiting me every Thursday

while the show was airing was a publicity stunt?" She turns around to glare at him. "Did it work?"

Mr. Geary has the good grace to look horrified. His face is white, his lips thin. His gaze flicks over to a display case. there are three Emmys and a Golden Globe inside it.

Mary guesses that it did.

Mary doesn't quite slam her hand through the glass door, but it's a close call.

Frey

"I was right!" Mary snarls. "Every script I sent you, every idea I had, I was right, wasn't I? You used them! I should sue you."

"You can't," Mr. Geary says quickly, almost too quickly. Like he was rehearsing it. "You were an employee of the production company. the scripts were our, legally."

Mary gasps. "You looked into it."

It isn't a question, so Mr. Geary apparently doesn't feel the need to respond. Instead, he shuffles his feet and picks at a cuticle on his left hand and says, "Maybe you sort of, absorbed the plot lines when you were in a coma? Crispin turned on the TV every time, made sure you didn't miss one episode. It could be that." He points to one of the bright yellow pieces of legal pad paper. "This, where she gets hit by the car, that was the Season Three cliff-hanger. I don't know how you know, 'cause it hasn't been aired yet, but...I could tell you how it ends?"

The girl of the week dies, Mary thinks. She gets tired, so tired, so when the car comes around the corner, she doesn't move out of the way. She just lets it happen. Because that's easier. At least, she thought it was easier. Now, she's not so sure. It was frustrating there, but at least it was predictable. Malleable.

Mary looks down at the desk and a photo catches her eye. She feels her face go white, all the heat and blood draining away, leaving her gasping for air a little. Mr. Geary follows the line of her gaze and quickly slaps a folder on top of the glossy.

"Malleable," she repeats to herself. "Manageable. Mine."

"Sorry? Did you want to know?"

"No," Mary says, but she's not sure who and what she's denying just yet. Her eyes bounce around the room, taking in everything and nothing, brain only processing little glimpses of snapshots, of red-inked scripts, of award trophies and videos marked "dailies" and new two-year contracts.

"No," she says again, and maybe she's denying that she had been living the life of the character they had shamelessly stolen from her while she was unconscious? that she had ever actually been there? Or that all her hard work, all her love for the series, still meant nothing to these people, that she still wasn't useful.

"Screw this," she says, and walks out of the office. If she's going to be exploited, then at least she's going to enjoy it. She's going to get something from it. At least she can really fuck up their plans. She's not going to be alone. She walks out of the hallway, out of the studio building, and onto the sidewalk.

Her name is Mary, and she has realized something.

She can't force Mark Geary to make the show better. She can't force Crispin to respect her. She can't force her co-workers to acknowledge her. She can't force Richmond to become more rounded, or to love her better, or to think for himself. She can't force Antonio or Sherri to be anything more than what they've been written to be. She can't force Night City to behave rationally. She can't force the constructedness of that world to resemble reality, and she can't force reality to be as perfect as a television show. But there is one thing she can do.

Her name is Mary... and she can finally take control of her own life.

She waits until the Craft Services van squeals around the corner before stepping out onto the street. She's not sure this is going to work a second time, but she has a good feeling about it.

"Malleable," she says to herself. "And mine. I win."

And back on the office, buried under a folder, sits an eight-and- half-by-ten glossy photo of the Mary Trinity actress in test vampire makeup. If Mark Geary had been paying any sort of attention, he might have seen it wink.

But probably not.

Acknowledgements

This story was originally conceived to accompany my Master's thesis, so I first have to thank my advisor, Doctor Jennifer Brayton, for letting me get as creative with my project as I did, and for encouraging me to pursue my creative writing outside of academia. My thesis was on the fanfiction trope known as Mary Sues (and Meta Sues), and I had a great time coming up with a story that plays so blatantly with the conventions of the genre.

A big thanks to Archia, who created the incredible and expressive illustrations of Antonio, Mary, and Richmond on the cover. I never regret commissioning her, and I am always delighted with how she interprets my characters.

And a massive thank you to Rodney, who put up with my Type A pestering and nitpicking like a champ. He is such a pillar of the Wattpad community, and has made my journey to starting my own imprint and self-publishing a smooth and enjoyable one. I don't know what I'd do without you, Rodney. Thank you so much for your patience and your attention to detail, and your generosity with your time and talents.

Gabrielle Harbowy, as ever, is the most brilliant woman, and I am always grateful that I have to good fortune to have her in my personal contacts listing on my phone. She gives the best advice.

Lastly, I have to thank the television programs and novel series of my youth that made me fall so in love with the vampire myth, fanfiction, and the vampire-as-detective-tropes, and whom I still desperately adore: *Dracula: the Series, Forever Knight, The Vampire Files, Angel: The Series, Dark Shadows, Moonlight, Nightwalker, Master of Mosquiton*, and *Blood Ties*. I satirize because I care.

--J.M.

Also by J.M. Frey

The Dark Lord and the Seamstress, a coloring storybook
"The Promise" in *Valor 2*
"Whose Doctor?" in *Doctor Who In Time And Space:*
Essays on Themes, Characters, History and Fandom, 1963–2012
"How Fanfiction Made Me Gay," in *The Secret Loves of Geek Girls*
"Time to Move," in *The Secret Loves of Geek Girls Redux*
"Bloodsuckers" and "Toronto the Rude" in *The Toronto Comic*
Anthology vol 2
"TTC Gothic" in *Amazing Stories vols 1-4*
Triptych
Hero is a Four Letter Word
The Woman Who Fell Through Time

The Accidental Turn Series
The Untold Tale
The Forgotten Tale
The Silenced Tale
The Accidental Collection
shorts and novellas from the series

The Skylark's Saga
The Skylark's Song
The Skylark's Sacrifice

About the Author

J.M. Frey is an author, screenwriter, and professional smartypants. She's appeared in podcasts, documentaries, and on television to discuss all things geeky through the lens of academia. Her debut novel TRIPTYCH was nominated for two Lambda Literary Awards, and garnered a place among the Best Books of 2011 from Publishers Weekly. Since then she's published THE ACCIDENTAL TURN SERIES, a quadrilogy of meta-fantasy novels, and THE SKYLARK'S SAGA, a steampunk adventure duology. Her Wattpad-exclusive queer regency historical fiction novel THE WOMAN WHO FELL THROUGH TIME was honoured with a Watty Award in 2019. Her life's ambition is to step foot on every continent – only three left!

www.jmfrey.net